WINGS

OF

FIRE

THE LAST PHOENIX: BOOK ONE

STEPHANIE MIRRO

TANNHAUSER PRESS

ALSO BY STEPHANIE MIRRO

THE LAST PHOENIX
Wings of Death
Wings of Winter
Wings of Magic
Wings of Life
Wings of Deceit
Wings of Mercy

IMMORTAL RELICS
Curse of the Vampire
Fury of the Gods
Revenge of the Witch
Rise of the Demons

COLLECTIONS
The Outsiders: An Hourlings Anthology

Dedication

For you.

"Hold fast to dreams,
For if dreams die,
Life is a broken-winged bird
That cannot fly.

Hold fast to dreams
for when dreams go
life is a barren field
frozen with snow."

- Langston Hughes

AUTHOR'S NOTE

Well, 2020 certainly wasn't the year we expected to have, was it? The Last Phoenix series was planned, and this first book written prior to the pandemic hitting the United States, where I live. After some consideration, I decided against updating the books to include the pandemic for two reasons:

1. It's easy enough to set the books in 2019 or even a few years prior.

2. More importantly, this is meant to be fantasy. A place where we can *escape* reality to worlds unknown and undiscovered, where vampires and witches and shapeshifters roam (and often terrorize the humans around them).

Writing this series turned into an escape for me as the writer, and I hope it can be the same for you. If it's not, my second go-to for an escape was a full glass of Merlot.[1]

So, grab a snack and something to drink and get comfy, because you're not going to want to put this book down.

Welcome to Miami.

---

1 Please drink responsibly. ;)

CHAPTER 1

Friday Night

I wasn't always the bad guy. I had a loving family once, all of whom I adored. My pulse raced as the grief tried to force its way out, as it usually did when I thought of the past.

The door of the sleek town car opened. Warm, wet air rushed in, caressing my cheeks and bringing my focus back to the present. I took a deep breath to steady my nerves—no time for a trip down memory lane tonight; I had a party to attend and goods to steal.

I took the driver's offered hand as I stepped out of the back seat, slipping a few bills into the man's palm. The trick was to leave just enough of a tip that the driver would be grateful, but not enough that I would be memorable.

Oh, who was I kidding? Any tip would be memorable. No one I knew even tipped these guys in cash anymore.

"*Gracias*," I said, sending my white-blonde curls back over my shoulder as I straightened.

"*De nada*," he murmured, his eyes widening.

I had entered the sedan's backseat in day clothes and emerged in a dress and heels, ready for the party ahead of me. The gentleman of a driver respected my request not to look in the mirror while I changed. His stare now was either the radical outfit change or the fact the front of my haute couture dress dipped to my navel in a waterfall of gold fabric, showing off the curves of my breasts.

Desired effect achieved.

After pulling my rather simple red masquerade mask into place, I was off to the ball. Or extravagant party, in my case.

My shimmering gown whispered as I walked across the burnt orange honeycomb driveway toward the front door of the Mediterranean-style villa. I always shopped for clothes with jobs in mind, which meant the dress's length and swishy fabric hid my thigh holsters with ease.

My looks were both a blessing and a curse. At times, I wanted to scream that I wasn't just a pretty face. But other times, including this evening, my looks paid dividends. For example, the man collecting the invites was too busy ogling my boobs to notice my invitation was fake.

Lucky me, right? Not that I needed luck; one way or another, I would have found a way in. The man's lecherous grin made me want to drop-kick him into next week, but no one ever expected someone who looked like me to have the secret life I did.

Or, rather, two secret lives.

I gave him a wink and a mysterious smile before heading inside. Miami wasn't shy about flaunting its homes of the rich and famous. The prices reached into the upper multi-millions, some even closing in on nine figures. The one I entered now on Star Island was no exception. The plastic surgeon who lived here, one Mr. Albert Renauldo, lived life to the fullest and loved to show it off. His need for displaying his fortune and subsequent fame worked quite well for me.

Because the truth was, I wasn't there for the party or to "ooh" and "ahh" over his pretty things, although I might have been alone in that. And I wasn't there to get in the man's good graces.

No, as it turned out, this was a heist. And not just any heist...

A supernatural one.

I'm Veronica Neill, Master Acquirer of the Fantastical. No joke, that's what it says on my business card. Though, technically, I leave my real name off and just use the nickname "Falcon." But no matter what you call me, the fact remains: I have a particular set of skills that make it easy to track down and acquire items with supernatural qualities that have fallen into the wrong hands.

I don't judge people when it comes to my contracts, so I can't say my clients' hands are any better. In fact, I make it a point *not* to look too hard into the person behind the contract. But the pay is good, *really* good, and the jobs? So. Much. Fun. With a little hint of danger on the side.

Like tonight. Here I was at a Miami masquerade ball with all the city's finest. Doctors, lawyers, singers, rappers, drug dealers—look, even a Saudi prince showed up. Name anyone with a lot of cash or a lot of supply, and they were here. Of course, there were also plenty of attendees with little to their name, hoping to score big tonight in one fashion or another.

As expected, I walked past the glass front doors, open to allow the night breeze to sweep through, and straight into opulence. Not like the place needed the breeze to cool it down—the air conditioning kept it at a comfortable enough temperature to keep guests from sweating too much in the endless Florida humidity.

The doors were open solely for show, another display of unfathomable wealth, and one reason I wouldn't feel guilty in the slightest when I relieved him of the fantastical goods he had hidden away.

The main living space had been cleared of furniture to become a dance floor, with a live band set up on one side. Sweeping staircases on the other side took guests up to even more luxury and drew the eye to the hand-painted tiles of the vaulted ceiling. From where I stood, an artist had molded fancy pineapples or even corn cobs into the tiles.

I squinted and tilted my head to the side. Hard to tell since I wasn't a botanist by any means, but smothered in gold whatever they were.

A crisply uniformed server approached me, balancing a tray of flutes as if it were nothing but air. "Champagne?"

I accepted the offered glass. "Thank you."

As he swept away to fill the next set of empty hands, I brought the champagne to my lips and took a sip, the bubbles tickling my nose. It certainly wouldn't be the first time I had a little bit to drink before a job. Not enough to get drunk or even tipsy, just enough to calm my nerves and loosen up. No matter how many jobs I took, the thrill of excitement never ceased, but jittery nerves could interfere.

Opposite the front entry, two more glass doors stood open, creating a cross breeze that mixed with the chill of the air conditioning. Just past the outdoor entertainment area and private dock, the view of the waterways and lights of the city took my breath away, as it always did.

Eager to be free of the eye-watering scents of overdone colognes and excessive hair products, I made my way through the crowd and out the back doors. I would have plenty of time later to enjoy the party itself if I wanted, but for now, the salty air called to me like a lover's scent.

The wind played a game of chase with my hair while I leaned against the railing, taking in the spectacular view. To my right stood the colossal condominium giants that made up Miami Beach. The fact those behemoths could resist hurricane-force winds and didn't sink into the ocean continued to amaze me. A testament to man's ingenuity. Little did they know that witches and warlocks helped keep those towers afloat.

The mainland stood to my left, just past another few islands and the MacArthur Causeway. Oh, and let's not forget the Miami Yacht Club. I wouldn't want to offend them. No, seriously, the supernatural Community members there were some of my best customers, both for stolen goods and a well-made latte or *cafecito*.

They never knew I did both jobs.

You see, when I wasn't pulling all-nighters at glamorous parties, locating and reacquiring fantastical goods for the Community, I lived my best life as a barista. People always threw me "the look" when they found out about my day job, giving me the "Oh… that's nice" phrase, as if they frowned upon my ability to make their fancy-ass drink du jour that cost more than a box of tampons. Maybe it was because I wasn't a high school or college student anymore.

Whatever the case, Veronica Neill's Instagram-worthy latte art made a damn fine cover for my real job, if I did say so myself, and I fucking loved all things espresso. Win-win.

"Gorgeous skyline," said a deep voice to my right.

I didn't need to look; I had already spied this delicious piece of eye-candy the moment I walked in. Everyone did. But I looked anyway, enjoying the man's features up close.

He had what I liked to call Prince Eric hair; you know the one, falls in love with a mermaid. It was that gorgeous shade of black that resembled the midnight sky between stars. Velvety, making my fingers itch to run through it.

Ay, papi.

His angelic white mask hid most of his features except his sculpted chin and his eyes. Those irises were definitely their own shade—a blue dark enough to look almost black until you saw them up close. Eyes that would be super easy to lose yourself in, as I found myself doing now.

"Enjoying the view?" His lips pursed ever so slightly as he smirked.

He knew he looked good. His black suit jacket hung open, pushed back slightly as he kept one hand casually in his pants pocket. The top of his white button-down shirt opened enough to display a gold cross hanging from a chain.

"I was enjoying the peace and quiet," I said, turning to face the water again so he couldn't see the flush rising on my cheeks. It wasn't a blush; losing myself in his eyes wasn't embarrassing. But I'd be lying if I said his whole demeanor wasn't an instant turn-on for me—no sense in letting a smug man like that see the physical evidence.

He leaned his elbows on the railing next to me. "You came to one of Dr. Renauldo's parties for peace and quiet?"

"You're telling me you didn't?" I glanced at him out of my periphery, enjoying the smirk my question earned. The man had deliciously full lips, and I wondered if they would taste as good as they looked.

I drained my champagne in one last gulp. I wasn't here for the kind of fun his lips promised, at least not until the item I sought was acquired, but that didn't mean I couldn't fantasize in the meantime. Maybe we could reconnect later in the evening.

"Are you here alone?" he asked.

I arched an eyebrow. "That's a creepy question, isn't it?"

"Not if I'm just trying to determine how good my chances are."

"Chances of what, exactly?"

"Of dancing with you." He took my empty glass and placed it on the flat railing. "May I?"

Without waiting for a response, he slipped his arm around my exposed back and ushered me toward the door leading back inside. Now, I normally wouldn't allow a man—make that anyone—to lead me around like that, as if they owned me. But this man's touch set my skin on fire, which was saying a lot considering what I am.

I wanted to feel more.

Inside, he swept me in a circle on the ballroom floor, my skirt whirling out around us, before pulling me in close for the slow dance starting up. The warmth of the room brought out the scent of cardamom drifting from the man holding me, a spice that suited him as well as his smirk. His palm pressed against the skin of my back. I could feel each of his fingers as if he were branding me. Scorching, and I craved more of it.

With the trumpet bugling out a solo, my wish was granted. The man lowered his head to place his cheek against mine, avoiding my mask with ease. A wildfire swept from my face down to my manicured toes. Something was different about this guy, and I didn't mean that in the falling-for-him, he-must-be-the-one kind of way. I meant he was something like me—a member of the Community.

Supernatural.

I pulled back to look into his eyes again, narrowing mine. "What are you?"

He laughed, white teeth shining in the light. Before he could answer, a woman brushed past me to place her delicate hand on his arm.

"There you are," she said, her green eyes flashing me a warning as she reclaimed what was hers. Except I wasn't so sure he knew that fact yet.

I withdrew my hand and stepped back. I didn't fight for men, but I wouldn't argue against men fighting for me. It seemed romantic and chivalrous. Too bad most men found me unapproachable. Maybe that was why this guy was so attractive; he had dared to approach.

"It gets so stuffy under these things." She lifted her tiger mask, and instantly, I recognized her.

It would be hard for anyone to forget this woman, with her flawless lily-white skin, almost translucent. She kept her auburn hair cut pixie length—a look that few could pull off as well as she did—which she had slicked back tonight for a dramatic look. The forest-green of her floor-length gown enhanced the sharpness in her similarly colored eyes.

Seeing her here, tonight of all nights, made my skin prickle with paranoia.

"Thank you for the dance," I murmured as I slipped away into the crowd, not allowing either of them to protest.

That was too close. If she recognized me behind my mask, this night could end badly—end up in a grim prison kind of badly. It was time to get to work before anyone caught on to the real reason I was there.

After waiting until the hallway leading into the bathroom was clear, I ducked inside. The powder room was more than large enough for what I needed. My dress was a two-piece: a floor-length, shimmering gold satin skirt attached to a matching, thin strap top that dove down to my belly button in front. The fabric still covered my ladies, thanks to a bit of boob tape, and left my back open to the breeze—and to scorching hot hands that made my body quiver.

Sonofabitch.

Without a further thought in *that* direction, I unhooked the skirt and flipped it over to its black satin side before tying it around my neck. With a quick flip, it would hide the golden top well if I needed it to and came down to my thighs. A suitable cape for my alter ego. Not that I was a superhero, by any means—quite the opposite. But it blended in well with this masquerade party.

The pants I had pulled on beneath the skirt were practically painted-on black leather that rode low on my hips and ended an inch above my ankle. My exposed navel piercing featured real diamonds, which would distract anyone from noticing that my top stayed the same. That was the goal, anyway. Flashy jewels, rich people, and gold diggers of any gender or species all went hand in hand.

I rearranged my toolkits, attaching them to the back of my pants and still hidden beneath my cape. The gun strap went in the trash, while the actual holster and gun clipped into my waistband against my right hip. I rarely needed the weapon, but it was better to be safe.

Last, but undeniably not the least, I removed and turned over my red mask, flipped up the back, and replaced it over my face.

I looked in the mirror. The somewhat sinister face of a bird of prey smiled back at me. Red, yellow, and orange feathers swirled together across the front, bringing life to the previously simple mask. Long, thin red quills flared out from the eyebrows, reaching above and behind my hair. Most people would only see the fierce face of a colorful falcon, which was exactly what I needed tonight.

According to my mother, the mask had been in my family for generations—as in thousands of years. I had to take her word for it, though. I'd never met any of my extended family growing up, and now all the family I did have were dead. My smile faltered as the heaviness of grief tried to rear its ugly head.

I closed my eyes and took in a deep breath, exhaling the memories with it. I'd grieved already, for years. Now it was time for fun. Making money at the same time was a boon.

So what if I was going against everything my parents ever taught me?

To complete the new look, I removed the fake brown contacts I wore to hide my alter ego, allowing my real violet irises to gaze through. The color was typically reserved for humans born with albinism, but my kind had a variety of hues, sometimes even several in one eye. Especially men.

After blowing myself a smooch in the mirror to calm my jittery nerves—my blood pumped with adrenaline as I readied myself for the job—I let myself out of the powder room and continued down the hall. The noise of the party faded away behind me.

I gave myself a wobbling step and a lurch here and there as I made my way up the stairs and around a few corners. Just a drunken partygoer on the hunt for the bathroom until a locked door indicated I had reached my destination. I hadn't spotted any cameras, but that didn't mean much in today's computer-oriented world.

"Falcon to Alley Cat," I said to the empty hallway, pretending to check something on my phone just in case anyone watched via hidden camera.

"You know I hate that name, right?" grumbled Kit's deeper, contralto voice in my earpiece. A sultry songbird if I ever heard one.

Katherine Parker—or Kit as she preferred to be called and suited her personality so much better—was my best friend and partner in crime. With thick black braids, the right side of her head shaved into a pattern that changed every few months, and more tattoos than I could count anymore, most people had no idea she was a technological genius.

She could also kick your ass faster than you could blink, thanks to her background in martial arts and obsession with weightlifting.

Never judge a book by its cover.

"How about AC?" I asked, barely moving my lips.

She muttered something into the earpiece before answering. "No. You find it?"

"Door's locked," I said. "Can you turn off any cameras?"

"Does Elvis still live?"

It was a rhetorical question. Kit was one of those people who believed the crooner's death was a government coverup and aliens had actually abducted him. No joke. Genius always came with a heaping side of crazy. That was why I loved the girl—she could handle my antics with ease.

"Done."

"You're the best," I said as I approached the door.

"You know it."

Setting the pins and opening the lock only took a few quick fiddles with my kit. I was sure Mr. Renauldo didn't anticipate anyone attempting what I was about to. I smiled at his foolishness, though the safe would likely be harder to crack.

For anyone else, anyway.

After one more glance around the hallway to make sure no one would see, I opened and slipped around the door, then shut and locked it behind me. Because it was night, turning on the office light was a big no-no as anyone enjoying the pool area would notice a sudden light coming on. Instead, I let heat signatures rise in my vision.

Oddly enough, the sweet scent of cherry blossoms filled the room, nearly suffocating in its intensity. My nose crinkled against the invasive scent. Not a smell I would have attributed to the party host, but who was I to judge?

Two chairs faced a wooden desk, a floor-to-ceiling cabinet of knickknacks stood behind it, and the safe...

...sat wide open and empty.

CHAPTER 2

Friday Night

Mother *fucker.* I was too late. Someone had beaten me to the jewelry box. For the first time *ever,* I had failed.

"People are headed your way, V," Kit's voice broke my slack-jawed stare. "You done?"

"It's gone." I blinked at the empty space where the box should have been.

"What? Shit. Well, get going. These guys might be part of the Community and look pretty serious. I think you've been made."

Cursing under my breath, I glanced at the window beside the desk, contemplating a different escape route. Keys jingled outside, deciding for me. Window it would be.

I crossed the room in silence and slipped open the pane of glass. A key slid into the door's lock and turned. I was sitting on the ledge of the window when the door opened, and two armed guards burst through. I winked in their direction before dropping.

"Stop!" a voice shouted from inside the office, which would have made me laugh for the absurdity of the command had I not already shifted out of my human form.

Had yelling at someone to stop ever actually worked for them?

In less time than it took to blink an eye, I had gone from woman to bird of prey, my human form and belongings waiting in stasis in some parallel dimension—the beauty of shifter magic in action. I flew to the nearest palm tree and landed on one of the fronds, trilling out my frustration at failing the job and almost getting caught in the process. The breeze ruffled the orange feathers on my chest, but the men at the window looking for me didn't notice.

In my bird form, I wouldn't be able to talk to Kit, but the blaring sirens and flashing red and blue lights pulling up out front of the mansion let me know the party was over.

Disappointment roiled within me, making my stomach clench. I dropped from the giant palm leaf and caught the wind, arcing out above the water before swooping back over the red-tiled roof. The bright hues of ultraviolet lights from this height made it easy for me to spot the humans as well as the smattering of Community members among the crowd. Each species had a distinct hue.

Then I spotted *him*.

Only it wasn't the ultraviolet light that caught my eye—it was the lack of it. He was devoid of color to my avian vision; instead, he seemed to leak darkness. Wisps of swirling shadows trailed behind him as he walked. The short-haired woman next to him, the woman I knew as Sophia, was the same.

Grim reapers.

Even with feathers to keep me warm, my body trembled in the air current. Why in Ognebog's blaze were they at this party? If they weren't there to collect a soul, then it had to be an enforcement capacity. Had someone tipped them off about me?

The two reapers slid into a vehicle to leave, and I veered away, heading back to my place. I needed to find out who had beaten me to the box and steal it back, or else I would be in some very deep shit.

MY ONE-BEDROOM apartment wasn't far from the coffee shop where I worked during the day, but the morning after the party and failed job, I needed to make a pit stop before heading in for my afternoon shift. Towering buildings cast plenty of shade in the morning hours, providing a small amount of relief from the oppressive humidity.

We took what we could get in a city like Miami.

Downtown on a weekday was congested, filled with honking horns and city bus air brakes. Businessmen and women dressed in suits or more casual linen slacks—the smarter choice for this heat, in my opinion—strode the sidewalks, each heading their own way and with a distinct sense of purpose.

On a Saturday like today, it was much livelier and full of color. From inside the more popular restaurants and bars, brass musicians belted out their Latin beats. As I passed open shop doors and windows, I enjoyed the fact that I didn't need headphones to keep me company. I never wore them anyway; it was too hard to hear anyone sneaking up on me, and in my line of work—my nighttime line of work, I mean—not hearing someone behind me could be a fatal mistake.

"*Oye, mami,*" a familiar voice called out. "When are you going to let me show you what a *Baricua* can do for you?"

"When you call me by my name," I called back to the dark-haired man, who crushed the end of his cigarette beneath his boot.

Because I took my job seriously, I already knew his name was Enrique Alvarez, a DJ at one of the hottest clubs on Miami Beach. He was tall, dark, and handsome to the T, and I'd be lying if I said I hadn't thought about taking him up on his offer. If nothing else, he'd be a great distraction from last night's reaper encounter, and I could all but guarantee he'd be a fantastic adventure between the sheets.

I sighed. Business was always getting in the way of pleasure.

"You never tell me your name!" he protested.

"Then I guess I'll never know what a *Baricua* can do for me." I turned and blew him a kiss before continuing on my way. His playful mutterings faded away.

A few streets later, I arrived at my destination. The little bell above the piano store door jingled in welcome.

"Veronica, you're back so soon?" asked a man's gruff voice behind the cover of a majestic black-and-gold grand piano. The music didn't even pause. Rhapsody in Blue, if I wasn't mistaken.

"You never are, my dear," Tony said, his dark brown eyes twinkling behind his thin wire spectacles as I rounded the piano. As a telepath, Tony was one of the rare people who knew exactly who and what I was. And as one of my favorite people on the planet, I would have married him years ago had he not been old enough to be my grandfather.

His coffee bean-colored cheeks and chin were as clean-shaven as his head, but grey hairs peeked out from beneath the top of his button-down polo. The shirt's floral pattern screamed its bright colors amidst the somberness of the black and white pianos.

I leaned in to kiss his bald black head, which shone in the fluorescent light. "Business, as usual."

He frowned up at me as I stepped back, his fingers halting on the keys. "The job did not go as planned."

"Nope." I shrugged, having long ceased to care about the invasion of my thoughts. At least when it came to Tony. I never received any judgment, only care and concern and sometimes caution. "But I'll work it out."

"Your client will not be happy," he said as he resumed his finger dance across the keys.

I bit my lip since I didn't have anything to say to that. Tony was completely right, and dread started to trickle its way up my spine. I'd been able to keep it at bay until then. Not wanting to let Tony see too much of my fear, I patted him on the shoulder and headed to the back of the shop, where a heavy velvet curtain separated the display room from the storeroom.

The curtain whispered as I slipped behind it. Not like a rustling of fabric—the barrier actually whispered my name as I passed through the veil, granting me access to the world hidden behind it. The piano shop was one of several entry points, but the only one I used consistently because of Tony. To most humans, the curtain simply kept prying eyes from seeing the clutter of the storeroom.

The world behind the curtain wasn't like another planet or anything, just a market for those of us without human genes or those humans granted an entry card. A place to gather, trade stories, and barter goods with like-minded individuals. But for me, it just meant business. I wasn't a loner by any means, but I made it a priority to keep my true identity hidden from just about everyone, and that meant avoiding friendships.

Sounded lonely, maybe, but I was the last of my kind. Priceless. A somewhat pretentious thought, but it was the truth I had to live with. I reserved my need for companionship to straight-up humans or as close as I could get to mortals, like my bestie Kit, who wasn't human but not quite immortal, either.

El Mercado Sombra, the Shadow Market, had been here for generations. No one I've met knew where it came from or who created it. But it was one of only a handful of its kind in the south, and it was a sanctuary. No magic could be cast here, other than that of the market itself, and no attacks could be made. Try, and *el demonio del mercado* would eat you up and spit you back out somewhere far away and wouldn't allow you to return. Some even said you got spit back out with missing body parts.

Or maybe that was just what they taught the kids to keep them in line. Either way, no one ever violated the rules.

Despite its name, the market was far from shadowy. The sun beat down here just as much as it did anywhere in Miami. As sweat accumulated and dripped down my back, I might've even argued that the humidity was worse within the market's confines because the surrounding buildings blocked the wind.

I strolled down the winding paved street, passing various stalls and carts, wishing I had time to stop and shop as I eyed some of the goods. Every once in a while, I found something I couldn't pass up, like the tiny glass sculpture of a mermaid I kept on my living room windowsill. When the sun rose, the rays would pierce through the glass and spread a rainbow of light across the room. I always associated rainbows with my little brother because he had loved them and everything for which they stood.

Sharp voices hawked their wares all around me, behind merchandise-ladled tables and beneath canvas tents. Sweet and savory aromas from the food vendors drifted beneath my nose, setting my mouth watering and my stomach grumbling. I hadn't eaten yet that morning, and I didn't eat enough after arriving home last night. Shifting forms expended copious amounts of energy.

Stopping at my favorite food cart, *La Bruja Hambrienta*, I ordered my usual: *picadillo cua cua*. I never understood how some people didn't like the taste of plantains, but for me, the mixture of the sweet fruit combined with beef hash, eggs, and served over rice was simply divine. I ordered it to go, planning to eat while I worked.

The girl running the cart today was new, and young enough to be the daughter of Manuel, the truck's owner. Probably his youngest daughter. I already knew the other two. Poor guy had his hands full with those girls. Maybe this one would go softer on him. When she handed me the plastic bag full of my food, I chuckled at the ridiculousness of that thought, earning myself a weird look as I turned away.

The computer lab was just across the street, another reason why the Cuban food cart had become my favorite. I found my empty desk at the back of the shop, facing the front, a place reserved for me so no one could sit behind me or see the screen. The owner and I had a financial understanding, and she didn't bother asking any questions once I told her the number that I was willing to pay for her discretion.

I set down my food and fired up the computer. In between forkfuls that set my taste buds singing like a choir of church boys, I pressed my thumb to the fingerprint reader, allowing me to log into the website used for setting up exclusive contracts. Some type of shadow magic secured the computer lab so well that no one could hack it, including the Death Enforcement Agency, making it uber-secure for people in my line of business. The website I used was technically illegal and existed on the dark web.

A message notification blinked on the screen. When I opened it, my appetite fled and threatened to expel the little I had eaten. I read it twice more after enlarging the text, in case my dyslexia was messing with me. No such luck—my buyer already knew I didn't have the box. With sweaty fingers, I furiously typed out a response:

X,

I understand your concerns, but please do not worry. You hired the best, and I don't fail. I need one more week to fulfill the contract.

Sincerely,

Falcon

I hit send while also letting out a whoosh of air I didn't realize I was holding. Failing this job would pretty much end my black-market career. Because everyone else my buyer hired so far was unable to find the item he sought, I had finally accepted his contract after the third request. A little bit of ego played a role in my decision—I never thought *I* would fail, especially not with Kit doing the research. She had found the damn box, after all.

But if the fate of the others after their botched jobs in our line of work were any indication, then future buyers would take this one failed contract as too big a weakness. It was a harsh, unforgiving business. And the most annoying part was that I didn't need the money; I just wanted the fame of obtaining something everyone else couldn't. If I didn't find that jewelry box fast, I was screwed.

And not in a good way.

I pulled up a message window and pinged Kit, "You on?"

"Always," came the swift reply.

"Can you pull up the mansion's camera feeds and check someone out for me?"

"Deets."

"A man and a woman," I typed. "Man is hotter than hell, woman is petite with short hair and wearing a tiger's mask. It's the woman, Sophia, I'm questioning. Did she go off-camera at all?"

"Gimme an hour." Her status went inactive. Kit preferred to work with zero distractions.

Sophia Clark wasn't a bad person, but boy did she and I get off to a rocky start a year ago. She was one of the few people who knew more than most about who I was, that the barista and the thief were one and the same. I still preferred to call it acquiring goods out of the wrong hands.

Regardless, we had both caught each other in acts we technically shouldn't have been involved in, and we had a mutual agreement to never speak of it again.

But it was rather odd that not one, but two reapers had shown up at the same party as me with no souls to collect. I hadn't known her to be my competition in the world of acquisitions; she was more into the buying side of things, rather than getting her hands dirty herself.

Then again, it had been a year since we'd crossed paths, and I already knew her moral standards weren't quite up to a promotion to the angelic choir yet. Her involvement wouldn't be a complete surprise.

Another message notification popped up, and I nearly groaned out loud as I read it.

Dear Falcon,

I look forward to the outcome either way. It would be such a pleasure to meet you, little bird.

See you soon,

X

My blood turned to ice, making my hands shake over the keyboard. The buyer known only as X was famous for his sadistic nature when his expectations weren't met, which was the main reason I stayed away from his contracts. I suddenly did not doubt he would hunt me down to the ends of the earth to teach me a lesson if I failed.

I may have made a *huge* mistake.

CHAPTER 3

Saturday Morning

I was just about to log off the computer when a bulletin on the Community forum home page caught my attention. It was a Most Wanted notice with...

What the actual fuck?

My picture stared back at me from the screen. Not like a headshot or an embarrassing old school photo, but a screen capture from a security camera. A close-up image of my phoenix masquerade mask from the night before.

They must have taken the photo before Kit killed the feed. With my mouth hanging open, I scanned the rest of the text. My pulse pounded in my ears. The DEA had declared the Falcon a suspect in a murder at Dr. Renauldo's party.

Wait, *murder*? Who the hell was murdered?

I sat back and covered my mouth with a hand, biting on my pointer finger to keep from screaming my frustration. I might be many things, but I was most certainly *not* a murderer. I had standards, damn it.

The reward from the DEA for finding and turning me in was…astronomical. I was being framed and in the worst possible way. But why? And by whom? I didn't even know who died. Maybe Sophia had recognized me beneath my mask after all. I wouldn't have marked her for a murderer, but I had been wrong before. Was she afraid I was going to spill the beans about her little side hustle? If so, she was going to regret her involvement, because I sure as shit wouldn't go down without a fight.

Things had gone from bad to really fucking bad in a matter of minutes. I pressed my fingers to my temples, pushing against the throbbing pain creeping in. Headaches, sometimes even migraines, were an unfortunate downside to using too much magic too quickly, but stress had become another equal opportunity annoyer. I was sure there weren't too many more stressful situations in life than being wrongly accused of murder.

Sweet Mokosh, what am I going to do? I groaned internally, not wanting to draw attention from the other patrons. Unfortunately, the mother goddess of the phoenixes didn't answer, not as if I really expected her to.

Kit would be offline for the next hour, so I had nothing to do but go to work. I could think during the walk, and the fresh air might help my headache.

MY DAY JOB SAW me at The Morning Grind, where I worked as a barista. The truth was, I'd probably keep the job even if I didn't need the cover. I was what I liked to call a coffee connoisseur, though some might use the term snob. Either way, perfecting images atop the light foam of a café latte was my form of heaven, and the dark brew beneath the foam was the nectar of the gods.

The coffee shop wasn't too far from the market, maybe a mile or so as the crow flies (or me in falcon form). Walking through downtown Miami would help me think through whatever the hell was going on. I let my gaze wander across unfamiliar faces, high-rises, and, because I always took Brickell Bay Drive, a glimpse of the water now and then.

Water of any kind always drew me in like a Siren's song, mostly because of the open air and salty sea spray. Above the ocean—hell, even just above lakes, rivers, and the everglades—meant soaring without worry. No buildings or trees to keep an eye out for, no people and their infuriating bird-deterring spikes to avoid when I landed on an island or a ship's mast. The ocean air currents down here in south Florida were some of my favorites to glide through, and one of the reasons I never left.

Unfortunately, the bulletin had me paranoid, making it far from my usual peaceful walk. A creepy-crawly sensation making its way down my back had me glancing over my shoulder every few feet. Nothing out of the ordinary caught my eye, but I would have sworn that shadows existed where they shouldn't. A crash behind me had me turning with fists raised in front of my face in half a second.

A man had simply dropped a box off a truck he was unloading, his curses filling the air. I gave a shrug and smile to another man giving me an odd look as I lowered my hands. Turning back around, I nearly jumped out of my skin when a beast loomed toward me. I stopped myself from kicking out at the last second when the sweet face of a German Shepherd panted up at me.

I was losing it.

The woman walking the dog pulled him away before I could pet him, glaring at me as she did. I couldn't blame her, though; I *had* almost kicked her dog.

Ugh. Today was not going well.

A line stretched from the register to the door of The Morning Grind today, which wasn't unusual. The coffee shop was long and narrow and tucked between a restaurant and a clothing store. Along with a handful of four-top tables taking up the back, a few two-tops sat by the front window and three stools tucked under the bar closest to the entry— all of which were occupied. The owner of the D.C.-based shop had gone for a rustic industrial look in Florida, so everything had that wood and metal look to it. Not quite my style, but I didn't hate it.

Some of my coworkers loathed the bar top stools and the closeness to the customers, complaining daily to our manager to remove them. But part of the whole barista gig was getting to know our regulars, so I took it upon myself to become the store saint by taking over the front espresso machine whenever I had a shift. Getting to know our regulars also helped me keep an ear on city happenings for my other job.

"Hey Joe," I said to one such gentleman as I tucked my purse into a storage cube under the counter. I pulled out a black apron and tied it around my waist. "How're Carmela and the boys?"

Joe grinned and lifted his espresso cup in a toast. "*Ciao*, V! They are well, of course. Just living the American dream."

Technically, his name was Giovanni, but he preferred to go by Joe to seem more American to Americans. Not that it made a difference, and certainly not in Miami. He was Italian through and through, from his beautiful black hair down to his always-polished Amadeo Testoni oxfords. His accent didn't help his cause either.

One of the most successful and therefore well-dressed businessmen I knew, Joe was also one of those regulars I talked about, stopping in almost every day, several times a day on occasion. By his own declaration and choice, he had become the unofficial Community Welcoming Committee of Miami. He had taken it upon himself to get to know me when I finally started venturing into *el Mercado Sombra* three years ago.

Joe and his wife Carmela had fled Italy after the war. Yes, the World War, but not because of Italy's involvement with the Nazi movement. No, they fled because their kind, the fae, was outed for a brief time in the country, hunted by humans both for their magic and from fear.

Xenophobia crossed species. Technically the word was speciesism, but I thought that sounded ridiculous.

It had taken a whole lot of magic to wipe all those human memories clean of a supernatural existence, which was a part of the reason why Kit didn't use magic anymore unless she had no other choice. Thankfully the Community had been vigilant about staying to the shadows ever since, making magic mostly unnecessary for Kit. I couldn't even remember the last time she had cast a spell or brewed a potion, other than the wards she set up around our apartments.

Joe's expression turned solemn, and he glanced around before leaning in. "Have you heard?"

My heart beat harder against my ribs, but I stayed nonchalant as I ground coffee beans for the next order. "Heard what?"

"Someone is killing my kind," he said just barely above a whisper.

While the news was sad, I couldn't help the slight release of tension in my shoulders. He wasn't talking about the wanted bulletin, which mentioned only one person who died at the party. I was sure Joe's mention had something to do with fae politics in the Otherworld, a topic and place I didn't really keep up on, but his kind always seemed to be having each other killed over something.

Never confuse the actual fae with friendly fairies.

I poured the ground coffee into the portafilter and tapped it to settle the grounds. "That's terrible. What happened?"

"A man like me," he said, with an emphatic gesture towards himself, meaning fae, "was killed at a Star Island mansion."

Well, fuck. Joe did mean the bulletin about me; he just didn't know it was about me yet. Wrongly so, I might add.

My skin prickled as goosebumps spread along my arms. Not only had they all but placed the murder on my head as the primary suspect, but now the victim turned out to be fae.

I hadn't even noticed that fact earlier—if it was mentioned at all—thanks to the shock of seeing my face attached to the crime. And why did Joe make it seem like the death wasn't a one-off deal? Maybe he had a lingering fear after the genocide he and his family fled. I hoped that was the case and there weren't more murders I hadn't heard about yet.

I had enough on my plate trying to track down this jewelry box before I became my client's sex slave or some shit if he caught up to me first. Now I would have the whole DEA looking for me, and if there were even more murders…?

I didn't want to go there.

After tamping the grounds into the filter, I raised it toward the machine with a shaking hand. It took three goddamn tries to get it locked into place.

Joe must have noticed, because he reached out a hand to cover mine. Having been raised in the human realm, Joe was a bit of an anomaly to the fae kind. Not the typical brooding, drag-young-maidens-to-bed-and-ravage-them-to-death kind I grew up learning about. Perhaps his Summer Court lineage played a part in his friendly nature. I'd have to ask him sometime when I wasn't distracted with unwarranted murder charges.

"*Stai attento,*" he said, giving my hand a quick squeeze.

I gave him a small nod as I steamed a pitcher of milk, waiting for the espresso shots to finish pouring, unable to say anything for fear of letting out a string of obscenities. Isaac, my boss, wouldn't approve, and he was only two feet away at the register.

After picking up his phone from the counter, Joe slid off the stool. "My clients await. *Arrivederci, bella.*"

I smooched the air twice in his direction as if kissing his cheeks from afar, then turned my attention to the steamed milk. The heart I made out of the foam was terrible, and it was one of the most effortless designs to learn. This whole murder situation had me spooked, and now it was affecting my day job. Goddamn it.

Do you know how hard it is to create art when you've nearly been outed to the Community and named a murderer? It's hard, even if it is just coffee art.

The rest of my shift didn't go much better. I dropped a mug full of steamed milk, breaking it and sending all its bubbling contents onto the counter in front of a customer. You can imagine how that went. After several more calamities, Isaac sent me home early.

My cheeks burned as I hurled open the shop's front door. In just over three years of working there, I hadn't had an off day. Not one. And this clusterfuck of a situation I found myself in had created the first. I rubbed my face, hoping the act would rub away the blush. I *never* blushed, and I *never* got embarrassed, and here I was, doing both like a prepubescent kid whose mom just kissed her in public.

After checking to make sure the street was clear, I jogged across to the other sidewalk, heading back to my apartment three blocks away. I needed to shower the stench of sour milk from my skin and change clothes before heading over to Kit's place to do some research. Her computer system and network were nearly as secure as the market's, but only by human standards. It would have to be enough for now, though, because I didn't trust going back to the lab just yet.

"Excuse me, Ms. Neill?" a deep voice I knew stopped me in my tracks. A voice that sent shivers up my spine as I remembered the delightful heat of his hand pressed against my back. I turned to face the reaper from the party.

Holy hell.

The man was even hotter in the daylight. And I didn't mean temperature this time, even if my internal heat rose as well. He had rolled the sleeves of his button-down shirt up to his elbows, and the muscles of his tanned forearm shifted as he lifted his arm to remove black sunglasses. His eyes stared into mine as if he could see into my soul. He probably could, considering his job title. His irises were a shade lighter than the sky at dusk, although not by much, and I lost myself in them just as easily.

His hair still resembled Prince Eric's, but today his face held a cruelty the prince most definitely did not have. It amazed me how *alive* he looked despite having died to get the gig he now held.

"Veronica Neill?" he asked again, a smirk pulling the corner of his lip up.

"Just V. And you are?"

He held up a badge. "Thane Munro of the Death Enforcement Agency. You and I need to have a chat."

CHAPTER 4

Saturday Afternoon

I knew I had been overly paranoid since finding the bulletin with my face on it that morning, but after speaking with Joe at the coffee shop, I realized I was paranoid for no reason. Very few people, reapers included, knew that Veronica Neill and the acquirer called the Falcon were the same person. I kept that list short, and there was a good chance this Thane guy had no clue.

Not unless the angels had gotten involved for some reason, but that was highly unlikely. They stuck to more critical matters like global warming and pandemics. Sophia was on her way to earning a set of angel wings, meaning she would be a fool to reveal my secret.

So, if that was the case, then what did he want to have a word about?

I already knew he was a grim reaper, one of the elite members of the DEA, when he failed to emit any ultraviolet light last night. But why was the agency sending a reaper to approach me on the street?

"You may speak," I said in a steady voice—quite the feat considering my racing pulse.

"This chat will be better suited at the agency." He motioned to an alley just a few feet up.

It took considerable effort, but I stopped myself from rolling my eyes or laughing in his face. You know, because walking into alleys with men you've barely met was such a great idea. At least it wasn't night, and I knew he had a teleportation device, otherwise his creep factor would be through the roof.

"Send me a calendar invite." I brushed past him.

"You were at Albert Renauldo's home last night," he said to my back.

I closed my eyes and bit my lip, but I didn't stop walking. "So were you."

"A man was murdered in his office," his voice followed me. "One of the fae."

I halted then and contorted my face into one of horror before turning to face him. Drama came naturally to me. "What?"

He smiled at me, that dastardly kind of smile that dampened my lady bits. When was the last time I had gotten laid? It might be time to take care of that, just *not* with a DEA agent. Dead guys weren't my type, no matter how good they looked.

"Terrible, isn't it?" he asked, though his tone made it clear it was rhetorical. He knew I was faking my response.

I mean, it was horrifying the fae had died, but it wasn't by *my* hand.

"Very. I wish I could help you, but I didn't see anything out of the ordinary. I left soon after you and I parted ways." Got to love the word soon. It made my statement totally true.

"See, that's the thing." He tucked his hands into the pockets of his crisp black slacks as he sauntered toward me. "We know you killed him."

Turned out the angels *did* reveal my alter ego to the reapers—the bastards.

I narrowed my eyes up at him as he closed the distance between us. "I'm telling you I didn't."

As I turned away this time, his hand stopped me—a scorching hot brand on my arm. Now that I was close enough to feel his breath against my face, the hint of cardamom mixed with the sweet citrus of bergamot and made my mouth water. Complex yet alluring. I looked back up, my breath coming out short.

"It's hard to forget eyes like yours," Thane said, lowering his gaze to my lips. "And those lips."

Fuck me sideways. Had I known someone would be murdered, I would never have gotten cocky enough to remove my brown contacts. The image the DEA displayed on the Community forum had revealed the color beautifully, which meant any number of Community members could connect the dots. Thank the gods Joe hadn't.

But now the man the agency sent, one of the most attractive men I had ever seen, was tempting me like no other.

He leaned in, his lips brushing against mine, setting off an inferno-like chain reaction that lit me to my core. I might have lost all my control and thrown myself at him, pulling him into the alley, had I not heard the click.

"What the—" I jerked my head back and looked down. Handcuffs secured my wrist to his.

The few people close enough to see us on the sidewalk continued by without stopping or even glancing our way. Reapers on duty had a sort of repelling reaction on humans, which made their jobs much less complicated by not drawing any unnecessary attention. Too bad the repellant hadn't worked on me with this guy.

"You're under arrest for the murder of Broderick Ó Faoláin and the theft of Albert Renauldo's personal goods," Thane said, his smile sinister as he reached his hand up to his ear. "I've secured the target. En route to HQ momentarily."

That motherfucking asshat. How dare he use my own desire against me. He had another thing coming if he thought he had secured his *target*.

The fire his touch set off in me was nothing compared to the actual living flame that writhed within me, even if his heat was the closest thing ever to come close. I called upon my inner fire now, focusing its attention on the cuff latched to my wrist. The metal turned white-hot within seconds.

When I pulled against the chain, my arm went right through the molten metal, not a mark left on my skin. The cuff fell against his pant leg, smoke rising as it burned a hole through the fabric.

He yelled and held up his arm, staring in shock at the dripping metal. Guess the reapers didn't know everything about me.

"I am *not* a murderer," I said, leaning sideways to kick him square in the chest as hard as I could. He flew backward and landed with a thud on the sidewalk, his breath whooshing out from the unexpected impact. I leaned over him as he wheezed. "And I didn't steal anything last night except a glass of champagne. You've got the wrong gal."

Before he could recover, I set off at a sprint, racing for the alley he had motioned to earlier and where I had been ready to drag him for some quick and dirty lovin'—before he tried to arrest me, of course.

As I ducked around the corner, his strained voice called out for me to stop and think about what I was doing. Instead of taking his sage advice, I shifted into my bird form, transforming in a heartbeat. I winged up to one of the three-stories-high roofs and settled beside some pigeons, who let out soft coos at the disturbance. My tiny heart thudded rapidly against my ribs, fluttering the bright orange plumage covering my chest.

That was way too close for comfort.

Thane ran into view a moment later, his face still in shock and his body casting light away from his entire being like a prism. If only I could see his refraction of light in my human form, then maybe he wouldn't be so tempting.

Seriously, who the hell was tempted by a reaper of all things? If nothing else, this encounter had squashed any further thoughts of the naked and sweaty variety.

Now, I just wanted to aim a kick right between his legs.

He raised a hand to his ear again. "Suspect is on the run." He paused as he searched through the alley, ending empty-handed at the back wall. Looking up, his gaze scanned the buildings and went right over me.

"Suspect has escaped. Method unknown."

If a bird could laugh, I would have done it. Avian shifters aren't very common, maybe even rare, so it probably didn't occur to him that I was up here. Other types of magic could have whisked me away just as quickly, after all.

I didn't want to draw any attention to myself, so I waited with wings tucked in while he pulled out his cylindrical teleportation device and activated the portal. Although the majority of my outer feathers were a brownish grey, allowing me to camouflage myself among the local bird population, the undersides of my wings usually gave me away if someone was looking for me. Shades of red, orange, and yellow swirled together, making my spread wings resemble a ball of flames.

When the teleportation circle disappeared along with Thane, I dropped off the roof and caught the warm current, flapping to gain altitude. I couldn't go back to my apartment close to the coffee shop; that was too risky now that someone had leaked my dual identities. So I flew to my safe house instead.

I landed on a penthouse terrace of one of Miami's tallest buildings, the Brickell Flatiron. A fancy perk to being one of the area's top acquirers of fantastical things was money. Lots and lots of money. Unlike some of my peers, however, I flaunted mine in private. I even donated hefty sums to

suicide prevention programs and support groups—
anonymously.

Even though the floorplan was smaller than some of
the others and I could easily afford larger, I'd chosen this
particular penthouse because it had a separate terrace off the
primary bedroom. Should I ever find myself entertaining
guests, no matter how fat a chance that was, it wouldn't be
difficult to hide my comings and goings. Practical. I even
kept a gilded birdcage in the room for appearances.

Also, this penthouse had the best view out of all of
them.

I shifted back to my human form, grabbed a cookie
from the jar I kept out on the kitchen counter for moments
like these, and stormed straight into the Italian marble
shower. I didn't even bother to remove my clothes. They
reeked, too. I shoved the cookie in my mouth, then turned
on the water as hot as it would go. I'd need to eat more later
because of the distance of my impromptu flight, but the
sugar would hold me over while I showered.

After my scalp burned from fierce scrubbing and I was
sure I had washed away all the day's sticky grime thanks to
the spilled latte, I turned off the water and wrapped myself
up in a fluffy towel. I glared at myself in the mirror.

"Stupid, stupid, stupid," I told myself. "You've gotten
reckless. Which is exactly what Mom and Dad warned—"

My breath hitched in my throat, and my violet irises
turned a darker shade, more of an indigo, as the grief crested
like a crashing wave.

That was just it. Mom and Dad were gone. Maddox was
gone.

I hung my head, letting my wet hair cover my face in shame. I was alone. My parents were wrong nine years ago when they said I was ready to become head of the household. I wasn't ready. I was barely eighteen at the time. Hardly capable of taking care of myself, let alone my brother Mad, too.

My hands gripped the sides of the blindingly white sink. I had failed him. My one job in life was to keep him safe, and I couldn't even do that. What I wouldn't give to hear my brother laugh one more time, or feel him curl up next to me when storms rattled the windows, or simply tell him that I loved him.

I took a deep breath and let it out slowly. Wallowing never did anyone any good, certainly not me. I pushed off the sink and into my walk-in closet, pulling out comfy terry cloth shorts and a tank top.

After grabbing a banana and my laptop off the living room coffee table, I made my way outside to the terrace where I settled into my chaise. To avoid hindering the view, the tower's architects had designed every terrace with glass railings. Watching the ocean change colors and fade to black as the sun set was a favorite pastime of mine, and it always soothed my unsettled nerves.

This evening was no exception.

I ran my fingers through my damp hair, allowing it to air dry in the salt-filled breezes, then opened the laptop. A message dinged as soon as my status showed green.

"You free?" read Kit's message beside the image of her smooth, topaz-hued face, courtesy of her Cuban and Dominican ancestry. The picture was taken right before she attended a local comic convention in costume last year, so she had done her black hair in dreads held back with a headband, going as some character from a zombie show.

"For now," I typed back.

"?"

"Long story, but the DEA showed up outside work. You see the wanted bulletin?"

"Fuck. Yeah I saw it, but how'd they know you were you?" she asked. "You know what I mean."

"I don't even know," I wrote. "But if the agency thinks I'm guilty, then I'm as good as dead."

"Bet you never thought you'd want a lawyer before today, huh?"

I leaned back and groaned. She was right. Never before had I wished the Community judicial system was more like the human one, with lawyers and fair trials. In our world, the agency's word was law because they were governed by angels, indisputably fair even if you weren't innocent until proven guilty. You were just guilty.

Hence, me being dead even though I was one hundred percent innocent for once. Angels weren't so indisputable now.

"What do you have on Sophia?" I typed, needing to move along before I wallowed too deep in self-pity.

A movement in the south channel waters caught my eye, too far even for my enhanced vision. I picked up the pair of binoculars I kept outside and held them up.

Just a seagull searching for dinner.

Mermaids swam close to shore every once in a while, and I had yet to see one in the scale. Contrary to popular belief, they didn't need the help of a sea witch to pass for humans. The few I'd met in the market walking around on two legs hadn't taken me up on my offer to see their tails. I even got strange looks like I was asking to see them masturbate or something. I needed to study up on my mermaid culture and etiquette—if I didn't get thrown in jail first.

Kit's message beep brought my gaze back to the screen. "Sophia never went off-camera and never near the office. Not even close. She only left the guy's side once to grab a drink."

"Did you see who went in to snatch the box?" I typed, then peeled my banana and took a bite.

"Not exactly."

"Witch, don't leave me hanging." I loved Kit like a sister, but her lack of communication skills drove me just about crazy sometimes. Okay, maybe more than sometimes.

"The feed was cut for exactly one minute, and whoever did it spliced it together really fucking well. I only noticed it on the third run through. But your friend was glued to Mr. Hotpants's side for all 60 seconds."

I chewed on my bottom lip, eyeing the clouds drifting by though not really seeing them, then took another bite of my banana. Whoever did this knew who I was and knew I would be going after the jewelry box. I understood competition, but the problem lay in the fact that I was not only being framed for theft, I was also being blamed for murder. I didn't leave clues behind, and I had a general rule in life not to murder people

It used to be a simple enough rule.

And one of the fae? Absolutely not. That was basically asking to be thrown in prison and tortured for the next few hundred years. Not my MO. Besides, there was no body in the office while I was there. Pretty sure there wasn't, anyway, but there *was* that overwhelming cherry blossom scent. Did the killer leave that behind to cover up or throw me off?

"Thanks, Kit. Did you check out the vic's background?" I asked.

"You sitting down?" she typed.

I groaned. Before I had a chance to reply, her next message beeped through, "Broderick Ó Faoláin, a Duke of the Autumn Court, specifically the Mac Tíre clan—one of the wolves."

Books and studying hadn't really been my "thing" growing up—that was more my brother's gig—but I knew she didn't mean werewolf. The fae organized themselves into various factions based on an animalistic hierarchy. Wolves were fairly high up, but only the Lions of the Summer Court or Bears of the Winter Court had enough power to become a king or queen.

Kit continued, "The Mac Tíre have been extremely vocal in their disagreement with the new Summer Court Queen, who wants to bring all fae back to the Otherworld. Rumor has it that the queen doesn't believe in mingling with those beneath their kind, which is everyone to her. One too many half-bloods as a result, I guess."

"So the queen had Broderick assassinated?" I typed.

"Seems like it."

It felt too easy and blaming it on me still didn't make any sense except as a coincidental scapegoat. Did my buyer have ties to the Otherworld? "What about the box? Can you look into that?"

I couldn't find anything on the damn thing when I did my own search before the party, and foolish me had shrugged and let it go. I could just slap that earlier me.

"On it." Kit's status changed to red once again.

I closed my laptop and stared out across the water, dark waves breaking gently against a multitude of docks. I finished my banana and set the peel on the small table beside me. Something about this whole mess wasn't right. A fae nobleman who opposed the queen had been murdered. That should be reasonably straightforward. Except his body was found in an office hiding a supernatural item that my buyer was willing to pay a hefty sum to possess.

Was Broderick after the jewelry box, or was he simply in the wrong place at the wrong time? Were the murder and theft even related?

What the hell did this damned box even do?

CHAPTER 5

Sunday Morning

I hadn't had a nightmare in well over a year, maybe even two, but the stress of everything going on brought them back with a vengeance. I sat up with a start in the dark, breathless, my hair and tank top drenched and stuck to my skin. The image of his limp wrist hanging off the edge of his bed, an empty pill bottle on his nightstand, seared through my mind.

I pressed the heels of my hands to my eyes, refusing to give in to the pain and grief that had consumed me for months after I lost Mad. Only Kit was able to bring me back to life.

Rain pelted against the windows outside as if weeping for my loss. That would have to be enough.

I swung my legs out of bed and checked the bedside clock—6:15 in the morning. Darkness still filled my room because of the storm sweeping through, which also meant the Shadow Market would be virtually empty. I'd need to risk a visit to the computer lab if I wanted a chance in hell at clearing my name.

Going to Kit's was out of the question; there was no way I would drag her into this mess any more than I already had. They weren't close, but she had family members to consider if things went south. And while she might be a technological genius, she was also a witch, and I was up against the FBI's supernatural equivalent. Maybe even the fae queen. Oi.

Speaking of the witch, my phone blinked with a waiting message from her: "No luck on the box. Whatever it is, the DEA is keeping a tight lid on it."

I grumbled at the agency's secrecy and her horrible pun, though I had a feeling she hadn't even noticed, nor would she care if I pointed it out to her. Kit was way too literal to get half of my jokes.

After splashing some water on my face, I tied my hair up into a messy bun, then pulled a dark hoodie on over it. My white-blonde hair, sometimes flashing hints of gold depending on the light, was too noticeable to be kept down.

I pursed my lips. Depending on how bad this situation got, I might even have to dye it. I grimaced. That would be a last resort.

I decided against sunglasses because they'd be too obvious with the gloomy skies, but I popped in a pair of brown contacts and applied a shit ton of smoky eye makeup. All-nighter chic, or perhaps even rocking the walk of shame.

On a Sunday morning in downtown Miami, the streets were often pretty sparse until the brunch crowd finally rolled out of bed. Today was the same, except add in the thunder and the pouring rain, and I was lucky if I saw another soul. I chose to enter *el Mercado Sombra* a different way than the piano shop so as not to draw any unwanted attention to Tony. He got plenty all on his own as a gatekeeper.

The Death Enforcement Agency had two primary jobs these days: collecting souls and policing the Community. It had started who knows how long ago with just collecting souls, then the agency became an enforcer of rightful deaths before it finally took on the role of keeping the Community safe and contained. Killing a member of that Community, and a fae of Broderick's distinction, was a huge fucking no-no.

I had basically topped the most wanted list overnight, and I still didn't know what they had on me other than the photo. But merely being in the wrong place at the wrong time didn't equate to murder. There had to be something else.

Because it sported illegally tinted windows—not uncommon in southern Florida—I drove my bright red Mercedes Benz to the parking garage, flashed a parking pass to the attendant through my cracked window, and headed down to lower level one. After finding an empty space, I parked and got out. The beep of the alarm ensured the expensive car would stay put.

A door on the far wall led to the sub-basement unless you were a Community member or a human with a pass. In that case, the magic read your DNA or barcoded pass and ported you straight to the market. Not only that, but this particular entrance dropped me off right next to the computer lab.

It paid to know all the ins and outs of a place. Part of my job as an acquirer meant getting as much information as possible about a place before going in, everything from blueprints to frequent visitors. Not-so-frequent ones, too. I had turned the same careful eye on the market before ever entering it. Back before I got careless enough to earn a murder charge, if that time ever existed.

I wasn't so sure anymore.

As predicted, the market street was empty due to the rain, all the tented stalls covered to protect the wares beneath, the food carts' windows closed tight. I ducked into the twenty-four-hour lab, surprised to see even one other person there. Like me, he wore a hoodie that covered most of his face with shadows. I guess we all had business to do, sometimes even on Sunday mornings before seven.

I took my usual seat, stuck my thumb on the reader, and logged in. Well, that's what should have happened. Instead, I received an error message stating my account was locked and to please call the DEA administration team for assistance. I rolled my eyes. As if that was going to happen.

Grumbling to myself, even though I'd had a sneaking suspicion this would happen, I stuck my pinky on the reader to log into my backup account. Tracing my first attempted login wasn't possible with the magically enforced security setup, even for the agency. I'd take the win, no matter how small.

Bingo. I was in.

Except the first thing to pop up was another bulletin. This time it warned the Community to cease and desist any and all dealings with one "Falcon," also known as me, and to alert the agency of any sightings of my whereabouts. The only bright side was that few people still knew that me, Veronica, and me, the Falcon, were the same person, and the agency hadn't outed me yet.

Putting my head in my hands, elbows resting on the desk beside the laptop keyboard, I rubbed my temples. The throb had returned.

My reputation was ruined. Even if—no, *when*—I straightened this whole debacle out, regaining the trust of the magical Community would take years. If ever. I had no idea how I was going to figure out who was framing the Falcon either. Or why. Sure, I had rubbed people wrong over the years. I succeeded at jobs where others failed. But was it really fair to fight fire with a goddamn nuclear bomb, like the DEA was doing to me?

You know who's a pro at figuring people out?

Not me, if my past failed relationships were any indication. I didn't really *do* people. What I did do, and really, really well, was track down stolen magical items. If I wanted to be nice to myself, items sometimes equaled people, but generally of the miniature sort like pixies and some of the lesser demons still able to come and go from the underworlds. I preferred non-breathing objects.

I spent the remainder of the morning researching Broderick and who would want him dead besides the queen. Turned out to be a long list. I didn't have the kind of time it required to look into each of them. But as I leaned back in my seat, about to throw my hands up and turn myself in, a lightbulb as bright as a camera flash illuminated my mind. I nearly toppled backward in the chair.

Thane. A reaper would have information about Community members and their enemies readily available.

Now to figure out how to corner him with no one else around.

CHAPTER 6

Sunday Morning

Before I confronted Thane, I needed to check the crime scene for myself. Okay, maybe I was also avoiding seeing the reaper again. Either way, I hadn't seen a body when I went into Dr. Renauldo's office. Even without turning on any lights, I should have seen a heat signature of some sort or smelled something decomposing.

I didn't experience either, which meant Broderick was placed there after I left, or he was dead in the room for hours. Like at least twenty-four hours to avoid detection by heat signature. Maybe that explained the strong cherry blossom scent I had noticed and promptly forgot until I saw my face on the wanted bulletin. I crinkled my nose.

The more I thought about it, I knew his body couldn't have been dumped there later—the Community bodyguards who showed up as I left would have noticed the lack of a body. They would have alerted the DEA of that not-so-minor detail once the body finally turned up.

Which meant Broderick had been in there all day, or killed and moved in during the party. Or maybe someone had bribed the bodyguards.

Shit. Someone was going to a lot of trouble and getting their hands very messy to frame me.

After logging out of the computer, I left my Benz at the garage and took to the skies. Star Island coming up. Flying in the rain wasn't my favorite—lightning could be even more of an issue for a bird and driving rain felt like repeatedly getting punched—but I also didn't want to run the risk of being tracked in my sports car.

Being able to shift into a sunset-hued bird came with a lot of advantages. Sneaking into a murder crime scene was one of them.

From my new perch on the wet palm tree frond outside the Star Island mansion, I could see into Dr. Renauldo's office, even through the rain. No one went in or out. In fact, the entire house appeared dark and empty when I flew around it checking for heat signatures before landing. The owners probably didn't want to stay in the place while it was still a crime scene. I wouldn't be surprised to see it on the market for sale soon. A million-dollar price tag plus the scene of a murder equaled a nearly impossible sell.

I almost felt bad for the rich guy.

It was now or never. I swooped down to the open office window, shook off as much water as I could from my feathers, and hopped inside. As soon as I shifted beside the desk, my clothes mostly dry besides my soaking wet shoes thanks to the whole internal flame thing, I knew why the window was left open.

I held my shirt to my nose, trying hard not to gag or heave from the stench. Either action would cause me to breathe in even more of the rot. Less than a second later, I found the source of the smell.

Behind the door, it looked like someone had splashed a can of red paint all over the walls, except it most definitely was not paint—just a shit-ton of blood. How the hell had I missed this, and what in Ognebog's flames happened here?

The taint of magic crackled in the air; my guess was the DEA hiding the blood from human eyes after a supposed "clean up." Fae blood could only be touched by another fae without magical repercussions, and I wasn't sure if the DEA had any fae on staff.

Had the real killer used magic to hide the body from me, too? Was that how I missed seeing him?

I pulled out my phone and called Kit. So much for not involving her. This was too big a deal not to get all the help I could. "Can you send me photos of the body at the scene?"

"You do *not* want to see those."

"So true, but I need to."

She sighed. "Fine, but don't say I didn't warn you."

My phone buzzed before we even disconnected. I opened the file she sent. Three photos in, bile rose hard and fast in my throat, almost too fast to stop. I closed my eyes and held a hand to my mouth until the feeling passed.

My throat burned with the aftertaste of stomach acid, but it was nothing compared to the horror that gripped my insides when I finally took another look at the photos. One by one, the images revealed the absolute atrocities committed against the poor fae's body. Who would do such a thing?

He had curled into a fetal position against the wall, his hand covering his eyes. Well, his eye sockets. The killer had taken his eyes out at some point. Gross. Crimson streaks stained his face like he had cried bloody tears. His chest had been opened, *outward*; his ribs had been broken and cracked, bent out and away from his chest, leaving a gaping hole in the center. His heart and other organs all appeared to be there.

But the worst part of the entire ordeal the man suffered through, the part that made me almost vomit, was on his back. When the police had moved his body, they found identical slices up the length of his back, inside each shoulder blade. Humans wouldn't know what that meant—they'd call it some weird serial killer statement or cult mark. But I knew what it was. Any of the Community would.

His wings. The killer had removed the fae's wings.

I swallowed hard, wishing I could unsee it all.

A deep growl snapped my attention toward the door where an enormous grey wolf stood, his head held low—a werewolf to be exact. His eyes shone an unnatural yellow, too intense, too *human*, to be just an animal. This particular wolf had to be at least one hundred eighty pounds of pure muscle. Not in his full bestial prowess without the full moon, but a fierce opponent, nonetheless.

"Greetings, Falcon," the wolf snarled out of a mouth not meant to make human words.

The ghastly sound sent shivers down my spine from how *wrong* it was. I knew werewolves could speak, but I'd never been privy to hearing it before. I wished I could go back to that time.

What I didn't know was whether this was a lone wolf or just ahead of his pack. There to collect the bounty on my head, I was sure, except for one thing. No one other than the angels, and now the reapers (and Kit, of course, damn the list was getting long) should know that I, as in Veronica Neill, barista extraordinaire, was also the Falcon.

Someone had leaked that detail, and now I needed to get the hell out of there.

As I backed up toward the window, my hands held in front of me to show I wasn't a threat, the wolf lunged, his jaws snapping for any part of my body he could catch. My training kicked in, and I threw myself to the side, his saliva sliding across my arm.

I rolled and leaped back to my feet. I could shift and fly away with ease; that wasn't the question right now. The real question was whether I wanted to make a statement or not, let the bounty hunters know who they were up against. My parents might have given their lives back to the sun nearly a decade ago, but that didn't mean they left a totally defenseless child behind, no matter how much I tried to convince myself otherwise.

And I had only gotten better since.

As he went after me again, I made the decision. Well, it ended up being a little of both options. I dodged his attack, spinning out of the way, then kicked him straight in the head.

The unexpected force knocked him sideways, and the wolf let out a whine as he slid across the wooden floor.

Before he could shake off the hit, I dove out the window and shifted mid-air. A risky move, but pretty fun, too, and now I had done it twice. Go me? My heart pounded in my chest as I winged my way up into the wind currents.

They knew who I was, and they were hunting me.

AFTER DOWNING A sleeve of Oreos, I was back on my penthouse terrace, pacing under the awning. The rain had let up some but not enough to hang out in, and I was too stressed to worry about eating healthy. Werewolves and who knows what else would be after me now.

I had determined they—meaning the bounty hunters, because I was sure more would come—knew that Veronica and the Falcon were the same, but that didn't mean they knew all of what I was. Not unless the angels chose to reveal that as well, and if they did, then I would be well and truly fucked. They must really want me caught, but hopefully not bad enough to reveal the last phoenix for what she was.

I needed more information, and for some reason, I hadn't thought of Sophia and her access to the reaper databases until that moment. Maybe because I'd much rather stare at Thane's face, and also because I didn't like her. Regardless of the reason, I would start with her.

"We need to talk," I messaged Sophia. Part of our mutual agreement included not contacting each other. Except that deal went out the window when the reapers revealed my alter ego to the Community.

"Come to the agency," she replied.

"Negative." The girl was crazy if she thought that was happening. I would out her so fast. I sent her a dropped pin to a nearby parking garage. "Top floor. 10 minutes. No one else."

"Fine." Sophia must have known I was serious if she didn't even try arguing. She was right on time, too.

After a quick flight over, I leaned against the concrete barrier of the roof, wanting to keep the open air at my back. Sophia and her big-ass polka dot umbrella approached cautiously. Somehow the little white clip controlling the front of her pixie cut did not suit her personality. She was almost petite enough to be an actual pixie, but I wouldn't mention it—yet. I would wait to see how much she pissed me off first.

I had gone for a baseball hat and a hoodie to deal with the rain-turned-light-sprinkle. But then, I wasn't wearing heels and a cute dress either.

"What." Sophia didn't even make it a question.

"How do they know?" I asked.

"If you're going to play vague games with me, I'm out of here." She started to turn away.

I ground my teeth together. "How does the Community know that I'm the Falcon?"

"Not from me, if that's where your tiny bird brain went." One of her eyebrows quirked up, her green eyes laughing at me. "That decision came from higher up."

"Why?"

"Because you're a murderer, Veronica." She glared at me.

I glared right back. "I haven't killed anyone, and you know it. You wouldn't be here if you thought that was true."

We had a few second glare showdown before she finally dropped her gaze to her impeccably painted nails. She really held onto human habits.

"What evidence do you guys even have?" I asked.

Her gaze met mine. "We found your hair on the victim's body."

My mouth dropped open. Even if Broderick's body had been in there before I went in, I hadn't gone anywhere near him. "How the fuck is that even possible?"

"You're trying to say you didn't enter the office even though we have witnesses who saw you leap out the window?" She arched an eyebrow.

"For fuck's sake, Sophia," I said, throwing my hands up in the air in exasperation. "I'm not disputing the fact I went inside, but I most definitely did not murder anyone. No one was in there when I got there, but they already emptied the safe."

"If you didn't do it, who did?" she asked, cautious curiosity in her voice.

"Help me find out." It pained me, even killed me a little inside to ask her, but having someone on the inside of the agency would be huge.

She paused before answering. "I can't."

"Why not?" A little glimmer of hope rose despite her words. She had hesitated.

"I know you think of me a certain way after our first encounter," Sophia said, grimacing at the memory, "but I'm trying to right that wrong. Helping you would only set me back."

"Tell me about the box at least. What the hell is it, and what does it do?"

"That would be helping you." She rolled her eyes.

As I opened my mouth to argue, she shook her head to stop me, revealing the small, tube-shaped teleportation device in her free hand. She sighed.

"I'll pretend we didn't have this little meeting. But that's as much help as I can provide. I'm sorry." She pressed the button on the device and stepped toward the holographic circle it created. Meeting my gaze with a sympathetic expression, she said, "I hope you find the real killer, Veronica."

A moment later, Sophia and her giant umbrella fizzled out of sight.

Fuck my life. I clenched my fists. I had managed to convince one person of my innocence, but that was nowhere near enough, especially since she wasn't going to help me. That left the only other option.

Off to see the reaper. Well, another one.

CHAPTER 7

Sunday Afternoon

Grim reapers didn't get time off on the weekends. In fact, they didn't even get evenings off. Their job was 24/7 because what else were they going to do with their afterlife? Besides, it wasn't like people stopped dying just so reapers could have a vacation. Although I'm sure that would be nice for everyone involved.

Reapers themselves remained in a sort of purgatory, an after-death limbo. The lives they had lived while still breathing weren't *quite* good enough to earn a spot in whatever heaven existed, but also not *quite* bad enough to merit a one-way ticket to the fiery pits of hell.

So the gracious god or gods, or whatever entity created the human world, had also created the Death Enforcement Agency as a way for these lost souls to earn their wings. As in their angel wings. That's right, boys and girls and everything between—grim reapers, including Mr. Tall, Dark, and Drop Dead Sexy, were destined to become angels if they played their cards right.

Their hopeful ascension to the angelic choir also explained why Sophia was so agreeable to keeping our mutually morally questionable antics to ourselves. If nothing else at this point, I could rule out her and Thane's involvement. From a purely physical standpoint, anyway.

Considering all this reaper knowledge, why Thane chose to keep an apartment in downtown Miami was beyond me. Holding on to the last vestiges of his mortality, I guess. Maybe he wasn't so different from Sophia and her pretty pink nails. Whatever his reason, I found his place after some online, black-market-style digging on one Thane Munro, deceased.

I perched on the windowsill of what turned out to be his kitchen, chirping in the early afternoon sun. The storm had finally moved on to terrorize some other Floridian townsfolk. Such was the way of life here. I waited fifteen minutes before determining the apartment was empty. Luckily for me, he had left a window cracked open to water his plant.

I was fairly certain that wasn't his intention, but it happened when the rain soaked everything in the vicinity, plant included.

One quick hop over the sill, and I shifted back into human form. I really had to hand it to my parents for forcing me to practice shifting for thousands of hours as a child. We didn't actually keep track of the hours, but it sure felt like thousands.

In the beginning, shifting forms was challenging to achieve and a bizarre feeling. When you shifted, the human-shaped part of you went to a static, parallel realm while your animal self came here. It was instantaneous when done right and relatively painless, barring those three panic-stricken days I had been stuck in bird form when I was seven.

I sat on the edge of the counter, letting my gaze take in the room now that I was on the other side of the glass. The kitchen was mostly barren, which made sense considering he didn't eat—the man was technically dead. Because of that, I was surprised to find a coffee maker plugged in on the counter with a bag of ground beans sitting next to it.

I crinkled my nose at the brand, but hey, who was I to judge? I just broke into his apartment. Our levels of bad taste were even.

I wandered through the rest of the sparse one-bedroom apartment, running my finger along the furniture and coming up clean. I had no idea how he paid for all of this, or why. It wasn't like he earned a monetary salary in his current gig. All his "earnings" went toward his wings, and his superiors—as in the angels—provided anything he truly needed. I finished picking through his empty drawers and closet, testing for loose floorboards, and searching under his bed and couch in under ten minutes.

I hadn't really expected to find anything useful other than the reaper himself, but I could hope for some luck. Maddox had been so much better at hide and seek type games than me.

My heart clenched at the unexpected memory of our childhood games. Letting out a sigh of frustration, I flopped down onto the couch and put my feet up on the coffee table. I tossed my arms over the back of the sofa right as the front door opened and the reaper walked in.

Enjoying his surprised pause a little too much, I gave him one of my disarmingly-charming smiles and said, "I've decided to forgive the handcuff mishap."

Thane's hand started to rise toward his ear.

"Now, now. Is calling for backup any way to treat a guest?" I hadn't moved an inch, but I let the threat ooze from my tone.

"A guest wouldn't put her filthy shoes on my furniture." He gave a pointed look at my soaking wet Vans, courtesy of all my outdoor antics that day, as he nudged the apartment door shut with his heel. It closed with a click.

I dropped my feet to the floor and sat forward. "I need your help."

Thane laughed as he shrugged off his rain jacket, hanging it next to the door. "The help you need isn't the kind I'm qualified to give." His eyes roved up my body until they met mine, a wicked gleam shining in those cold, midnight blue irises. "Unless you mean something a little more carnal."

I scoffed, my lip curling up. "Ugh, gross. I'm not into necrophilia."

Not that I knew of, anyway. My body might have been trying to tell me otherwise with the warmth accumulating between my legs. I ignored it. His kind and my kind did not mix well in any romantical sense. His type was sterile, and I had a sacred duty to perform…someday.

Getting my mind back on track, I said, "I didn't murder anyone."

His eyes narrowed at my insult, but he chose to ignore it. Maybe he was smarter than his pretty-boy looks suggested. "So you say."

"It's the truth, and I need your help finding out who actually did it."

Thane took the chair across from me and steepled his fingers in front of his face. His elbows rested on the arms of the chair. "Why should I believe you?"

"Have you seen the body?" I asked, trying really hard not to visualize the images Kit had sent.

"Unfortunately."

"Do you think I'm capable of that?"

He tilted his head to the side. "I don't know you well enough to say what you are or are not capable of."

"Maybe not, but come on. His ribs were broken in the wrong direction, like from the inside out. And his..." I paused, swallowing a lump forming in the back of my throat. It was difficult to say out loud. "His *wings*."

He narrowed his eyes again. "You don't know, do you?"

"Fairly certain I've already said I don't know who killed him." I wasn't sure how he would take it if I suggested he get his hearing checked.

He smirked. "You don't know that his soul was stolen."

My eyebrows shot toward my hairline. "Are you fucking serious?"

"Taken while he was still alive."

Holy shit. I figured the DEA was involved because of the death, but I never even considered a crime of this magnitude. Stealing someone's soul was like... Well, like nothing else. It was incomprehensible to the supernatural Community.

Add in the fact that the victim was a fae of noble blood and the killer had removed his wings, and we had complete and utter blasphemy on our hands.

CHAPTER 8

Sunday Afternoon

I stared at Thane's face, noting the lines of his chiseled jaw and Romanesque nose. Not overly long like the Romans were often depicted, but perfectly sculpted. It took me a few heartbeats to realize he was smirking at me again. The knowing kind. Knowing I found him distractingly attractive.

In reality, the sacrilege of stealing someone's soul—and while that person was still alive—wasn't something I wanted to discuss in detail, nor was I prepared to even think about it. Focusing on his features kept me grounded in the here and now, like studying a piece of fine art. I could also tell he knew my surprise was genuine, which worked in my favor.

"So, are you going to help me track down the real soul stealer?" I asked when I found my voice again.

Thane leaned back in the chair. "No."

"Why not?"

He shrugged. "Not my job."

"Isn't it your job to make sure souls end up where they're supposed to be?" I asked, urging my voice to remain calm despite my growing irritation. I was starting to understand why he hadn't earned his wings yet.

"Yes, but my role in this matter is to bring you in. Another team is searching for the soul."

Time to try a new tactic. "Don't you want the glory of bringing the killer in?"

He considered me for a moment, the gears turning in his mind almost visible behind his eyes. "I want the box."

"The stolen one?"

Thane nodded. "The jewelry box in exchange for my help."

"What does it do?" I asked, my curiosity piqued. "I couldn't find anything when I dug through DEA records."

He simply stared at me.

Either he was about to enter a life of crime and sell the box to the highest bidder, thereby all but forfeiting his wings—if he got caught—or there was something about it I didn't know. I felt like I was walking into a trap, but no other options presented themselves at this point.

I put my hand out. "Deal."

Amusement danced across his features like a well-played fiddle.

I immediately started second-guessing working with such a good-looking man. My impulse control was terrible. I would just have to keep reminding myself of what he was—dead.

"We don't need to shake on it," he said. "I'm a grim reaper; my word is good."

I kept my hand out and waited.

With a dramatic eye roll, he leaned forward and slipped his palm into mine. The scorch was instantaneous, setting me ablaze in all the best and worst parts. As a child of the sun, I didn't feel heat the way others did. If anything, it was more of a comfort than anything, and fire didn't do a damn thing to me.

The fact that I had such a strong reaction to his touch intrigued me.

So, I didn't shake his hand to seal the deal—I knew what he said was true. Everyone in the Community knew their word was akin to their god's. But I needed to see if I had imagined the heat of his touch the other night.

I hadn't, and now a deliciously tempting throb pulsed between my legs. I bit my lip and dropped my hand before I was tempted to act on it.

What the hell was this guy doing to me, and did he feel it, too?

"Okay, partner," he said, a glint in his eye. "Where do we begin?"

"First off, don't call me that," I said. "Second, I need coffee." Coffee would help keep my hunger at bay until I had a chance to eat. I didn't usually shift as often as I had lately, and it was starting to catch up to me. I rose from the couch and made myself at home in his kitchen. "Third, we need to get you better coffee. This stuff is terrible."

He chuckled from his seat, not bothering to get up and help. So much for chivalry.

"Why do you even keep coffee?" I asked, filling the carafe with water from the sink. I'd have to hope the machine had a filter. "Or an apartment, for that matter?"

"Why do you care?"

"Care is too strong a word," I said, pouring the water into the machine's reservoir. "We're going to be working together, and I'm curious."

"We all know what curiosity did to the cat."

"Ugh." I shot him a look. "Seriously, tell me why you keep an apartment."

Nothing but silence as I replaced the carafe on the burner. I rolled my eyes. So that was how it was going to be.

"My mother," he said.

Not quite the answer that I expected. I glanced at him out of my periphery, but he hadn't moved. "Does she live here?"

He chuckled again, a pleasing sound that promised a good time. "No. She continues to pay my rent."

After scooping out the grounds with the supplied spoon, I started the machine and then turned and leaned my back against the counter to face him. "Why?"

"In the hopes that my spirit will use it." His eyes met mine, but his expression was too challenging to read. "So, I do."

Interesting. I wouldn't have pegged him for a momma's boy or even sentimental. The sweet smell of warm earth rose from the filling carafe. "For how long?"

"A while."

This was like pulling teeth. "Where's all your stuff?"

"She donated it."

"How does she afford it?" I asked.

Thane tilted his head to the side. "That's pretty personal, don't you think?"

"Do you not like talking about it or something?" I asked with an exasperated huff. I found an empty and surprisingly clean mug in the cabinet above the coffee maker and filled it with coffee.

"Would you like discussing the details of your own death and its effect on the people you left behind?"

I cringed. Ouch. He had a point. I sat on the couch again, this time with a full mug. "Okay then, new topic. What do you guys have on me?"

"Veronica Mirilla Neill, also goes by Falcon." He grinned when I rolled my eyes. "We know you're a shapeshifter, though of what kind is classified. By your nom de plume, I'd guess bird."

I held in my sigh of relief so he wouldn't see it. At least the angels didn't share the truth of my existence with just anybody. I had no idea where Thane stood in the reaper ranks, but based on this apartment, I'd bet he was still pretty new. Then again, people weren't my specialty.

"Funny. Way too obvious, though, don't you think? Falcons are really good at figuring out problems, they're fast, and they're sturdy. Seemed appropriate for my alter ego and doesn't have much to do with my species." It wasn't *exactly* lying. I was so much more than just a shifter. "I want what you guys have on me."

He shook his head. "I've already looked through your file; there's nothing in there that will help this case. I know your parents died nine years ago, that your younger brother was killed three years ago, that—"

"Wait, what? Mad died by suicide."

"Not according to your file."

It felt like someone knocked the wind out of me. I couldn't breathe, my mind frozen in this space and time, his words echoing in an empty chamber.

Maddox had been *killed*?

CHAPTER 9

Sunday Afternoon

I realized after a moment that Thane had continued with whatever nonsense he was saying about my life.

"Who killed Mad? And why?" I interrupted, not caring how rude it might have seemed.

"That part was also confidential." He eyed me. "You honestly didn't know?"

"No." My voice came out as a whisper.

For the last three years, I had blamed myself for Maddox's suicide. My brother was eight years younger than me, still in high school by the time I had finished college and moved on to a corporate job. Mad struggled in school, especially because I was gone so many hours of the day for my job, not to mention all my late-night partying and drinking binges. I was big into the club scene, trying to numb my anger and fear after our parents left the world.

But I told myself all teens struggled, that his behavior was normal. He would be fine.

I had been so wrong. I didn't know until after he was gone that some classmates had bullied him. Not just taunting and name-calling, as if that would have made it better somehow. No, these three assholes had bruised his body anywhere that could be hidden by clothes and even broke a few ribs. All because Mad and his boyfriend had displayed their affection to each other in the school halls.

When I found out all of this—his additional injuries on the autopsy report required an investigation—I took revenge. I had donned the phoenix mask for the first time and taught those boys a lesson they would never forget. That wasn't just bravado talking, either. I checked in on them from time to time, made sure they remembered my promise to them.

After that, I quit my corporate career, hating that I had prioritized it above my family. Kit helped me discover the job I do now as a means of channeling my anger and frustration. The extra funds also allowed me the opportunity for atonement by donating to suicide prevention groups.

But even knowing Mad had suffered for months because of these three boys, I should have known. I should have seen it, should have been there for him. Looking back, I knew he had tried on more than one occasion to tell me about the bullies, but I was always in a rush to get to the next exciting party or client meeting. My anger at our parents for leaving me in charge had fueled my life.

How could they have left me responsible for my ten-year-old kid brother when I barely knew how to keep myself alive?

Sure, I could fight. They made sure of that. But I needed them. Mad needed them. I don't care how long they had lived, how tired they were, or how much Dazhbog called them to return home to the sun. I had spent years feeling like they failed us, when really it was me who failed them.

Thane cleared his throat, and I raised my glossy gaze to his face. "You're about to spill your coffee on my couch."

And this was why I didn't date the guys I picked up in places like bars and fancy Star Island house parties. Just because they made for excellent eye candy and delicious romps between the sheets did not mean they would be suitable life companions. Not that I wanted any of that from Thane, but it was usually the opposite with party boys. In fact, I had yet to be proven wrong.

What I needed right now was a fucking hug, not criticism about my cup holding ability or lack thereof. So what if I spilled coffee on his couch? I had just found out my brother didn't take his own life, that he had been *killed*. And I had no idea why or how or any other details. How about some patience with a heaping side of sympathy?

At least his lack of empathy helped me wrestle my emotions back under control.

Raising an eyebrow at him, I tipped the mug a little further, letting the black brew collect at the edge. "You mean like this?"

He leaped to his feet, his hands outstretched to stop me. "What are you doing? That's Italian leather!"

"Calm the fuck down," I said, righting the mug and taking a sip. "You sound like my mom."

My heart seized at my comment, and I almost choked on the coffee. I wished my mother could lecture me again. All those little things I thought I hated about my parents? Now I would kill to see or hear or feel any of them just one more time.

But I was all alone, the last of our kind, the last phoenix. And unless I started procreating sometime soon, there would be no more. When I finally returned to the sun in another five hundred years or so—or, the more likely scenario, got killed in my line of work—my kind would be extinct.

It was far from the right time to be thinking about continuing my species; I needed to save my ass first. Time to stuff my feelings back into the corner of my mind and get back to business.

"Okay, so who would steal a soul?" I asked Thane when he finally sat on the chair, though he kept his eyes on my mug. I was tempted to tip it again, just to be a prick, but I restrained myself with great effort. I did say drama came easily to me.

"If I knew that, we wouldn't be here, now would we?" he asked.

He was turning out to be so much more annoying than I initially thought. "We wouldn't be here at all if you reapers could do your jobs right."

"I—" he started to argue.

"We don't have time for this," I snapped, glad to feel something other than pure desire for this man. "What can you tell me about souls?"

Thane rubbed at his chin, which was free of any scruff.

I wondered if he could even grow a beard in his current state. I wouldn't think so considering he was dead, just like vampires couldn't, and I was pretty sure angels couldn't, either. Or maybe just didn't. I didn't actually know what angels could and couldn't do, except fly and ruin my life.

"Those who are deep in the black-market side of things know the energy of a soul can be tapped into," he said.

Now we were getting somewhere. I leaned forward. "Tapped into how? For what?"

"The energy is essentially siphoned into a container which can then be used as a catalyst in spellcasting."

"Witches or mages?"

"I've heard of both, but the theft of a soul is rare and very difficult to do," he said.

I set my mug on the coffee table and pulled out my phone. Perusing my list of names, I ended up highlighting three, which included two witches and a warlock. No mages, unless they kept their hatred of the fae a secret. All three on my list had an issue with fae nobility, particularly the victim.

"Alright, I've got three possible suspects." I handed him the list.

There would be more names if I ruled out a connection with the victim and it had been nothing but poor timing that got Broderick killed. Except my gut told me they were connected somehow. The guy would have had the worst luck imaginable to simply be in the wrong place at the wrong time.

He read over the list of names, his eyebrows lifting. "You've been busy."

"You try being blamed for a murder you didn't commit, almost get arrested by the DEA, then get ambushed by a werewolf," I said, counting them off into the air.

He handed my phone back. "If you had just come along to the agency, we wouldn't have had to blow your cover."

I rolled my eyes and stood. "I'd be charged and beheaded right now if I had just 'come along to the agency.' I've got a contact in the witch community. Let's go."

"Are you forgetting something?" he asked, eyeing the coffee mug I left on the table.

"You visit your old apartment and keep coffee," I said. "If you're that big on wanting to feel alive again, you can do your own goddamn dishes."

I MESSAGED KIT that I would be showing up with one piece of eye-candy in tow, but I failed to let her know *how* we'd arrive. It wasn't really my fault, though, because I hadn't known beforehand.

Traveling via teleportation was not as enjoyable as I thought it would be. In fact, the experience felt a bit like every part of my body, every molecule of my entire being— even the wrinkles of my fucking brain—got pulled apart, rearranged, and put back together again somewhat haphazardly. Like my parts didn't get put back where they belonged.

There was a very good reason why only the reapers used teleportation devices.

I stumbled out of the circle and fell to my knees, a hand clamped over my mouth in case the vomit came all the way up. I got lucky, and the acid just stung the back of my throat and made my eyes water. Lucky for Kit's rug, too.

Thane regarded me with pure amusement dancing in his eyes. The bastard. He knew, and he hadn't even warned me.

"Need a trash can?" asked Kit's familiar deep voice from her bedroom. A moment later, she walked into view, drying her face and hands on a towel.

I didn't know why she did even that much; she was sweaty from head to toe. Dressed in little more than a bright green sports bra and black short shorts, it was clear she had just finished a workout. Exercising—correction, lifting weights and practicing karate were as much Kit's passion in life as were all things tech. I had always assumed her shorter stature played a part in her desire to stay fit, but it was also probably due to not using magic anymore.

Her near-nudity also gave Thane a great view of her body art, most of which was displayed on her brown skin at the moment. Her entire right arm was sleeved already, covered with her favorite sci-fi quotes and images from books and shows. Not being a sci-fi geek myself, I couldn't even begin to explain what they were. One looked like a blue British police box, which didn't make much sense to me.

I shook my head to answer her question, then immediately regretted and second-guessed the decision as my world rocked and spun.

"It'll pass in another minute," Thane said.

"I'm guessing you're Mr. Tall, Dark, and Deadly?" Kit used the towel to dry the shaved part of her head and under her braids.

"Guilty." His wicked smile suited his answer. He also failed to hide his appreciation of the view her lack of clothing provided. His eyes took her in like she was a feast waiting to be served.

"Cute," Kit said with zero humor in her tone. She flicked a hand toward the two folding chairs she had set up next to her workspace in the corner of the living room. "Take a seat."

Kit's apartment was a compact one-bedroom, despite my many attempts to buy her a bigger place. Not only did she get half of everything I brought in completing contracts, but she was also the heir to her family's fortune—a family of powerful witches and warlocks that could be traced back several millennia. She could easily afford better on her own commissions, but she didn't want anyone else's charity. (Her words.)

She had left her family and coven decades ago and was happy where she was. I had learned to stop pushing.

When she raised her murphy bed, a metal bar holding a punching bag came down, and her bedroom doubled as a fitness studio. A pile of weights, bars, and kettlebells lined the wall under her third-floor window. Nothing fantastic to see outside, however, just the wall of the next building over. Maybe I should start pushing her to upgrade again.

Thankfully, Thane had been right; the awful sensation of having my body parts rearranged faded within another minute. I followed him to Kit's desk and sat in the empty chair.

Much like her sculpted body, Kit's tech setup was a work of art. Four monitors displayed just about everything she needed when doing her research, connected to the world's fastest computer, which she had named the Hubble. Something to do with cosmology or astronomy or something. I tended to glaze over any geek or tech talk.

"Give me the list," Kit said as she pulled up a database with just a few clicks.

As I read off the three names, she typed each into the search bar and had their nearly complete Community dossiers open within seconds. Her files wouldn't be quite as thorough as the DEA's, but they would give us what we needed.

Thane whistled low.

Kit shot him a glance. "What happens at Kit's, stays at Kit's."

He held his hands up in a sign of surrender. "I'm just impressed. The agency's system is much more cumbersome to use."

"Dead guys aren't exactly tech-savvy, huh?" I enjoyed the glare my comment earned. Speaking of death seemed to be a sore spot for him. He hadn't been super enthusiastic agreeing to help me, so I didn't feel too bad taunting him.

Kit typed a few more things into the system. "One of the witches has an alibi for the time of the theft. She wasn't even in Florida."

I crossed that name off my list, leaving two.

"The warlock will be the most difficult to track down," she said, her dark brown eyes tracking through a variety of open files and windows on her screen faster than I could follow. "He tries to stay off-grid. The witch has a shop in *el Mercado*."

"What kind of shop?" Thane asked.

Kit turned a blank stare on him before looking at me with a raised eyebrow. "Is he newly deceased?"

I snorted as I tried not to laugh. She wasn't being rude or sarcastic, even if Thane didn't know that. She was just being Kit—super literal.

His cheeks reddened and his jawline moved as he clenched his teeth. Before he could open his mouth to retort, Kit moved on.

"She sells everything one might need to brew a potion or cast a spell," she said, pulling up images of the shop to show him. "Herbs, mortars and pestles, cauldrons. Whatever you think a witch might use, she's got."

"Alright, so we'll go visit her while you track down the 'lock." After getting back to my feet, I grimaced as my stomach flip-flopped from the sudden movement. "I'll meet you there this time."

Thane shook his head. "One rule: you don't leave my sight until we catch whoever is responsible."

CHAPTER 10

Sunday Afternoon

I glared at the reaper. If he tried to handcuff me again, he would be an even deader dead guy. "You've got to be joking."

Thane smirked. "You'll get used to teleporting. Eventually."

"I don't plan on getting used to it," I said, my neck flushing with anger. "I'm not the suspect anymore."

"Not to me, but you are to the agency," he said. "I can't protect you if you get caught when you're not with me."

"It's a good thing I don't get caught," I huffed. "And I don't need protection. Just your position."

"And what position would you like me in?" he asked with a gleam in his eye.

"V, stop arguing and get going," Kit said. "He's right, and you know it."

I sighed and motioned to Thane to start up his device. "Fine. But if I throw up, I'm aiming for your shoes this time."

When the holographic circle appeared, Thane reached over and took my hand. Once again, his touch set my palm ablaze, forcing me to look up to his eyes. This close, the deep ocean blue of his irises sparkled as if mixed with tiny flecks of silver. Stars in the night sky. He pulled me closer, holding me to his warm chest, his arms wrapped around my back. The hint of lavender vied with the spice of cardamom, curling around us. The sweet aroma settled around me and eased my anxiety.

A shiver ran up my spine as his fingers brushed my skin through my top, and the image of him caressing his way down my body, setting every inch of me on fire, invaded my thoughts. My body betrayed me, pressing itself closer to his.

A moment later, he dropped his arms, and I nearly crumbled to the ground. My insides heaved, but not enough to make me feel sick almost to the point of throwing up this time. When I shook my head to clear it, only a slight tingling sensation made itself known before fading away.

I looked up. We were in *el Mercado Sombra*, just outside The Witch's Brew. The shop's neon sign—a stein bubbling over with a potion—glowed in the window. I really needed to get myself one of those teleportation devices, just sans its tracking ability, and only after I got used to the jumps.

Thane held open the door. "After you."

I guess he had some gentleman-like tendencies hidden deep down after all. I stepped inside.

My senses were immediately assaulted by the smells, colors, and clutter of the place. Crystals of all shapes and sizes and every imaginable hue were randomly scattered across shelves or tossed in baskets, right next to relics, animal charms, and miniature statues of various gods and goddesses. I wasn't sure the owner's madness had a rhyme and a reason, or she was just lazy.

Some larger items like bundles of reeds, firewood, and brooms leaned against walls or anything else relatively stable. I didn't think the brooms were for flying, though. Kit never mentioned being able to fly.

Witches and warlocks were different from mages in that they were genuinely supernatural, living longer than average lives compared to humans. This longevity explained how Kit lived through the second World War and the fae outing incident in Italy. Witches and 'locks drew their magic from the elements, and it usually came as naturally as breathing for them.

Mages, on the other hand, were humans who learned to use magic, including the shadow arts like necromancy. No one born into the Community would stoop so low. I tried not to judge them all for the acts of a few, but sometimes it was difficult.

Regardless of how their magic came to be, all three needed catalysts and conduits to store energy for use in bigger spells, or for when their own magic reached critical levels. Like with most things, energy—magic in this case—was finite and required time to replenish.

I passed a few jars with questionable contents, including two labeled "Eye of Newt" and "Tongue of Salamander." I swallowed hard, trying to ignore the queasy feeling still plaguing my stomach.

This shop seemed to provide anything magic users could need and more to cast even the most strenuous spells. I really didn't know much about this kind of magic, although it wouldn't hurt to learn how to store some of my own someday. Kit didn't really like to discuss her magical prowess, and she was the only one I felt comfortable talking to about it all. But she preferred her tech skills to potions and powders, claiming computers were more reliable.

I tended to disagree. Anything techy always broke in some way for me, but Kit convinced me that was user error. She was most likely not wrong.

"Greetings, seekers," a voice intoned from the rear of the store. A beaded curtain hiding the backroom spread open of its own accord with a tinkling sound similar to tipping a rain stick, and a woman glided through the opening, carrying a large brown packing box.

Even though there were no wrinkles on her flawless skin, bronzed like the desert sand, it was easy to tell she was one of the old ones. Power emanated off her in waves, almost visible in its intensity. The air around and behind her blurred in its wake. Her hair, the rich color of a leopard and as glossy as satin without a single speck of silver, blew back from her shoulders as if moved by a gentle breeze.

That was the other thing about witches and warlocks—their magic grew in strength as they aged. Supposedly mine would, too, but no one I knew could confirm that now.

"Are you Luciana Pérez?" I asked as I approached the counter that she stood behind.

"I am," Her voice had a lilting, almost lyrical quality to it, and her smile was honest as she set the box on the counter. "It's a pleasure to meet you, Ms. Neill."

Her gaze flicked to Thane, hesitating before giving him a quick nod.

I wasn't sure how I felt about her knowing who I was until I remembered my face had been plastered on a giant bulletin for our world to see, and my name leaked for bounty hunters. Most of our Community was somewhat wary of the reapers, but I found it an odd response from someone as powerful as her. I had assumed she could strike him down with a flick of her wrist.

"Can we ask you a few questions about your relationship with Broderick Ó Faoláin?" I asked. No sense skirting around the issue.

"Of course, but I can also save you a lot of time." She cut through the tape sealing the box and pulled out the crinkly paper that kept whatever was inside safe. "I didn't kill him, and I didn't steal the...whatever he was after."

Despite the topic at hand, I gave a small smile. I liked anyone who got right to the point.

"You know what it was," Thane said, his tone blameless but interested.

She didn't meet his gaze; instead, she pulled out an empty, clear mason jar from below the counter and set it next to the box. After reaching over to the nearby Cricut machine, she peeled off a label and stuck it to the outside of the jar.

"Of course. *Tanets angelov* is well known to my kind," Luciana said, "but only a handful of us knew its most recent location. It should have been safe there."

She lifted a smaller, white box out of the large shipping one, holding the container as if the slightest movement would shatter it into pieces. She placed the box on the counter, very careful not to disturb it.

"What does that name mean?" I guessed the words were Russian or some sort of Slavic language.

"Why would the fae want the jewelry box?" Thane asked before she could answer my question.

I glared at him.

Luciana raised a knowing eyebrow in his direction before returning to her task. "The same reason anyone would want it, I suppose. There is a disturbance in the fae realm. An uprising. Many are not pleased with their current political state and seek a new option."

When she opened the small box, a glittering white light came from within. Using a pair of wooden tongs, she gingerly lifted an item out—a dice-size cube of compact snow that reflected light as if the sun shone down on it.

"The *tanets angelov* would give them a new option," she said.

I was absolutely sure the cube wasn't used to chill any drinks. Unable to resist, I asked, "What is that?"

"Snow from the highest reaches of the Otherworld," she said as she placed the cube in the mason jar. "The fae queen allows us to use it in conjuring."

"Conjuring what?"

"Ice guardians," she said as if it were the most ordinary answer in the world. In our world, it was.

"Broderick Ó Faoláin's soul was stolen," Thane said.

Luciana's head snapped up, her dark brown eyes sharp and focused on him. "Then it was not another fae. Not only is it sacrilegious to their kind, but their earth magic lacks the ability."

"Which is why we've come to you," he said. "How do we know you didn't take the box and the soul?"

"I was here that night. You may check the security footage." Luciana tilted her head behind her toward a camera high on the wall. "You know magic cannot tamper with the feed in *el Mercado*." She continued to pluck cubes from the small box and place them in the jar. The light coming from the box slowly diminished as the cubes transferred to the new container.

"Besides," she said, looking up to wink at us, "if it had been me, you both would be dead by now."

Thane cracked a rare smile. "It's possible."

"You need to speak to the only other person on your list," Luciana said.

My skin crawled with paranoia from her level of knowledge about our investigation. Was she lying to us? "How do you know who's on our list?"

She smiled as she met my gaze. "We are a family, we who come from the elements—a *close* family. Very few are capable of removing an individual's soul. I know you have already ruled out Maria, which leaves the warlock Rogelio, whom you'll find deep in the cup at the bar, On the Rocks."

"You think he's capable of theft and murder like this?" Thane asked.

"No, but I believe he will lead you closer to the answer."

"What do the three of you have against the fae nobility who want to stay here, anyway?" I asked.

Witches and warlocks weren't human, but they weren't fae either, although both were pretty damn close to immortal. Witches of either gender were their own supernatural species with their own form of governance. Why they cared what the fae did was beyond me, but these three were on my list because of their open and fervent display of disgust for the current fae court's opposition, those who wanted the fae to remain in the human world.

"The 'nobility,'" she said, crooking two fingers in the air, "like Broderick have been infringing upon this realm for too long. They seek to keep their kind among the humans. However, they won't listen to reason, and I am afraid it will come to war if they continue."

I didn't understand what she meant by infringing unless she had a thing against half-bloods. I might not be good at the people side of life, but something told me that wasn't the case. Luciana didn't seem like the type to care about the result of who slept with whom, especially considering magical abilities were a dominant genetic trait and almost always passed down to half-human offspring. In some rare cases, the magic didn't even dilute.

"War with whom?" I asked.

Luciana met my gaze, sorrow deep in her expression. Her next word sent goosebumps up my arms.

"Everyone."

CHAPTER 11

Sunday Afternoon

Even though Thane and I were traveling instantaneously via t-port device—which, yes, did get easier on my stomach each time—stopping by the victim's place of residence sparked our mutual curiosity. The DEA had already done a thorough sweep of Broderick's home, but they were convinced the killer was me. Knowing what we did now, Thane and I decided to take another peek around for anything that could help my case, while also bringing a crazed killer to justice.

Giving the warlock more time to drink at the bar could make his tongue even looser. A win all around.

We stumbled to our feet—well, I stumbled, Thane landed perfectly poised—in front of the door. Considering the fact that Broderick had been a duke, I expected him to live large like Dr. Renauldo. Instead, his house was in Morningside, a gated, upper-middle-class neighborhood. Expensive, but not overly extravagant.

Palm trees sprung up in every yard, towering over the homes. Their large fronds provided bits of shade and relief from the sun and stifling humidity for anyone spending time outside. Lush green grass extended over every bit of ground not otherwise covered by cement, brick, or stone. The neighborhood was close to Biscayne Bay, so fresh breezes brought in a hint of salty sea air.

The house was more modest than I expected considering the million-dollar price tag it must have cost. A grey, Spanish-style tile roof covered the white-and-brick exterior, and matching grey shutters hugged every window. It was quaint and peaceful, and I was sure many people would be drawn to such a place, escaping to their own private oases in their backyards. But I much preferred the bright lights, noise, and general busyness of downtown.

To each their own.

"Ready?" Thane asked.

I nodded, and he placed his palm on the middle of the door. The lock clicked, and the door swung open before us. The place was warded by the DEA to only allow agents inside, and it accepted Thane's request to enter. Like I said, I knew it would be super helpful to have a reaper on my side, and I loved being right.

The house was lightly furnished, and pristine, as if the victim never replaced the staged furniture when he bought the place. As was becoming more common these days, a faux wood tile covered the floors, making sandy escapades that much easier to clean. White plantation shutters covered every window, tilted open slightly to allow a bit of natural light inside.

Thane went to the right, toward the open-concept kitchen, so I headed left toward what I assumed would be bedrooms. Each of the three smaller rooms and the primary was sparse and immaculately kept. Did the guy actually live here, or was this all for show?

I didn't get much time to wonder.

Murmuring voices close to the house pulled me to the window, which offered a decent view of the gravel driveway. A group of four well-dressed men and one woman approached the front door. From where I stood, I couldn't tell whether they were humans looking to buy a home not even up for sale yet—also known as vultures. I unlocked and opened the bedroom window a few inches before moving to the door, staying hidden.

"Thane?" asked a man's tenor voice, surprise evident in his tone.

"Your Highness," Thane replied.

Your Highness? I peeked through the crack in the door just in time to see the reaper bow. The other men in the group blocked my view, but the tips of their pointed ears confirmed my suspicions. The fae prince had arrived.

Shit.

"Why are you in Duke Ó Faoláin's home?" the prince asked. "I thought the agency had already done their search."

"They did," the reaper replied. "I am pursuing my own hunch."

"Is that right? Tell me more."

Two of the fae broke off from the group, scanning the details of the house. One headed my way, and my skin prickled with paranoia. The prince must have sensed something off about Thane's response. That or he was looking to cover something up before the reaper found it. Either way, me getting caught would put a serious kink in our day's plan.

"The girl charged with murder has been difficult to catch long enough to bring in, and she adamantly claims her innocence. I'm starting to believe her."

Starting? I stopped myself before I snorted. He better have said that just for the prince's sake. I inched back toward the open window, then shifted into bird form and landed on the sill. As the guard stepped inside the room, I flew away. The front door was still open, so I swooped down to the ground beside it and hopped closer.

"...opposed to your beliefs that fae kind belongs solely in the Otherworld," Thane said. "I suspect that someone who agreed with you acted alone or on your queen's behalf."

"That's quite a bold accusation," the prince's tone was icy. "Do your superiors know of your little private investigation?"

I had missed part of their conversation during my quick flight, but it sure sounded like the prince didn't want Thane poking his nose around the murder. Interesting. I couldn't think of anyone more guilty at this point. Now we just needed to prove that the fae prince murdered one of his own and took his soul somehow, or he was acting on behalf of his queen. Great.

"Not until I have some concrete evidence," Thane said.

"Ah, of course. You do realize fae are incapable of performing such atrocities, yes?" the prince's voice lightened to almost cheerful.

"That doesn't mean the killer didn't get help from outside the fae kind."

The prince sighed, a bit dramatically if you ask me. "No, I suppose you're right. If you'll excuse us, Adam has granted us sole access to the house to perform a cleansing."

"As you wish," Thane said, his voice tight with what I assumed was annoyance or embarrassment at being dismissed. Footsteps tapped against the tile, coming toward the door.

I flew to the corner of the porch and shifted back to my human form just as the reaper stepped outside, his t-port device held in one hand. He pushed the door shut and looked around, presumably for me.

I let out a quick, low whistle to get his attention. When he rounded the corner, anger radiated from him like an overworked boiler. The magic portal appeared with the push of a button, ready to whisk us away, and we obliged.

A whirlwind of a moment later, Thane deposited us in an alley. My stomach grumbled in response but didn't send anything up. At the end of the alley, I recognized the busy lanes of the A1A. That and the strong smell of salt in the air confirmed we were close to the ocean—Miami Beach.

"I can't believe Adam approved Edric's cleansing request so soon." The lines along Thane's jaw moved as he clenched his teeth.

"Who's Adam? And what's a cleansing?" I asked, feeling like I had done myself somewhat of a disservice by not following fae politics more. Or fae anything, it seemed.

I managed to connect the dots that Edric was most likely the prince's name, but I mentally kicked myself for not paying more attention to my lessons. I had always preferred physical activity to books.

Thane leaned against the alley wall and crossed his arms. "Adam is my boss, and a cleansing is a ritual that removes any trace of the fae kind from a dwelling, not just blood. Any chance we had at finding evidence at the house pointing to the queen, Edric, or their followers will be gone."

My hopes sank. Just when I thought we were getting somewhere with the fae prince's arrival and shady behavior, he went and scrubbed the place clean.

"Let's hope Rogelio can provide some insight." Thane pushed himself off the wall and headed for the street. "Either he's working with the fae or he knows someone who is."

CHAPTER 12

Sunday Afternoon

Anywhere else in the city, Sunday afternoons saw a wind-down of the bar crowd, so I was surprised when On the Rocks turned out to be packed. Located on Miami Beach, it attracted an eclectic clientele, but Rogelio was still easy to spot from his stool at the counter. The warlock shouted obscenities like I'd never heard before at the football game playing on the TV behind the bartender.

It wasn't the obscenities that caught my attention, though.

Rogelio Diaz wasn't nearly as powerful as Luciana, nor did he seem to care as much about keeping himself from aging the way the other witch did. Still, power dripped off him like melting butter. The man must have been a few centuries old, but with elemental magic running through his blood, he would only appear sixty or so to the human eye.

A thick salt-and-pepper handlebar mustache reached past his chin, and a Panama hat sat atop his black hair. He kept his mint green linen shirt unbuttoned at the top, allowing a good amount of coffee-and-extra-cream-colored skin and wiry chest hair to play peek-a-boo with any ladies or gents daring enough to look. The opening also allowed a fabulous view of his plethora of tattoos, creeping all the way up his neck to his chin.

He glanced our way as Thane and I approached, his glossy gaze drinking in my tanned legs before settling on Thane. Fear filled his eyes, and he muttered a curse before bolting.

Neither of us expected that sort of response, but we wasted no time pursuing the warlock as he aimed for the back door. I'd made a smart choice wearing Vans that morning.

Luciana hadn't been wrong when she said the man would be deep in his cup, but she failed to mention he'd flee or fight back. She might have also been wrong about him being guilty. Why else would he run?

We caught up to him in the back alley. He crumpled against the dumpster after tripping over his own feet.

"*Invoco fuego,*" he said in a slurred voice as he held a palm out toward us.

A spiral of fiery magic appeared in his hand and shot toward me, although I had an inkling he was aiming for Thane. I caught the fireball in one hand, tossed it into the air, then swallowed it like I would a piece of popcorn or candy. The warlock gaped at me, as did Thane. Maybe he still didn't have access to my entire file.

I burped, and a smoke plume drifted out of my mouth. Whoops.

"*Demonio*," he murmured, crossing himself. Witches and warlocks might have been created from the earth's elements, but that didn't stop them from following human religions and superstitions.

"No demons here, Rogelio," I said. "But I've got some tricks up my sleeve, too. Why did you run?" I avoided looking directly at Thane, but his intense stare made the hairs rise on the back of my neck.

Rogelio's gaze, which was no longer glossy, slid to Thane. "I'm not ready to die."

The reaper rolled his eyes as he refocused his attention on the warlock. "What do I look like, a banshee? I'm not here to foretell your death. We're here because of Broderick Ó Faoláin."

Rogelio struggled to his feet, using the lip of the dumpster as leverage. He brushed off his clothes. "Well, why didn't you say so?"

"Because you ran," I said.

"Ah, *sí.*" Rogelio righted his Panama hat, which had fallen askew. "How can I be of service?"

"Do you have an alibi for the night of Broderick's death?" Thane asked.

The warlock narrowed his eyes at the reaper, apparently no longer afraid of him. "You think I had something to do with the murder?"

"I mean, you ran when we showed up, so yeah," I said with a shrug.

He waved the comment off with a hand. "You must understand how it feels to see one of Death's own show up at your door."

"You're at a bar," I pointed out.

He shrugged. "Same difference."

"So, where were you that night?" I asked, putting my hands on my hips as my irritation grew. I most definitely was not cut out for questioning suspects and witnesses.

"Here." He twirled the ends of his mustache with his fingers.

"Someone can confirm that claim, I assume," Thane said.

"*Sí*. Ellie was on shift that night. Speaking of which, I'll be heading back in to finish watching the game."

Thane leaned against the bar's back door, keeping it shut. "Not yet. Broderick's soul was stolen."

The warlock's face paled, and he crossed himself again. "Blasphemy."

"Right. So who would want the *tanets angelov* and a fae's soul?" Thane asked.

"Oh, ho ho," Rogelio whistled low. "This keeps getting better. *Tanets angelov*, eh? Someone is after a big payday."

"One of yours?" the reaper asked.

Rogelio narrowed his eyes. "*We* would not stoop so low."

"Who would?" Thane pressed.

"There are only a few others capable of such a task and would do so without remorse," Rogelio said. "The demons or the vampires."

Thane sighed. "I know that much. I need names."

I glanced at the reaper. I sure hadn't known other Community types were capable of such a feat. Did he assume I already knew, or was he keeping that knowledge from me on purpose? Either way, the 'lock's response made sense. The fae queen could have been working with the demons or the vampires.

The fae kind's earth magic was capable of controlling lesser demons who lived in the upper levels of hell, closer to the earth's surface. Only the demons who had risen among their ranks and subsequently sunk lower beneath the earth's outer surface were bound to remain in their own realm. A fae queen would have more than enough power over a demonic minion. She could easily force it to do her bidding.

Vampires were equally as likely a possibility because fae blood was fatally poisonous to the bloodsuckers. It would be in their best interest to have all the fae return to the Otherworld as soon as possible, just as the current fae queen seemed to want.

Rogelio shifted from foot to foot, his gaze darting around the alley. "I could get killed for giving you names."

"You could get killed for not giving them," Thane pointed out.

Whoa, whoa, whoa. I frowned in his direction. No one said anything about killing anyone. Torture, sure, but I had standards. Then again, if it helped clear my name, I might be willing to look the other direction. He'd be doing the killing, after all, not me.

"You said you weren't here for my soul," Rogelio protested, putting up his hands and backing away.

"I'm not. Scary thought, isn't it?" Beside me, Thane grew larger and darker, shadows drawing close to cling to his body. Menacing energy lashed around him, and his eyes became deep and hollow. "Where would your soul go if it wasn't collected?"

Rogelio fell to his knees and pressed his palms together in supplication. "I only know of two in this area who hold enough power to take a soul. The demon Mammon or the Master Vampire of Miami."

I held in a snicker. He certainly didn't take much convincing.

"Xavier Garcia," Thane said, returning to his usual human-looking self within the blink of an eye.

In the next blink, my stomach curled in on itself as pieces clicked into place. Xavier. X. The man who held the contract I had yet to fulfill was a vampire, that much I knew. But was it possible that he wasn't just any old vampire, but a *Master* Vampire?

My mouth went dry. The truth had been right in front of me the whole time, and I had missed it in the utter chaos that had become my life.

I glanced at Thane. I might have promised him the box in exchange for his help, but I valued my freedom and my life higher than a promise. Talk about sloppy. I hadn't known exactly who X was until now, just that he was a sadistic vampire I didn't want to cross. Weren't they all, though?

Because of that naïve line of thinking, I hadn't done a thorough enough background check on him. I had been too focused on the fame of succeeding where others had failed. I had gotten too cocky and ended up taking a contract from the Master Vampire of Miami.

Wow, that was the dumbest mistake I'd ever made. Maybe my last.

I swallowed hard. There was no way I could give Thane the box with this knowledge. But I didn't know what the hell the box did besides hold jewelry. I'd assumed it had some sort of magical protection imbued into it to keep the contents safe from theft. Seemed I was wrong.

How could I have been so stupid? More importantly, could I really give an item of such immense power, an item that could turn the tide on fae politics and start a war between realms, to a Master Vampire?

CHAPTER 13

Sunday Afternoon

After Thane gave Rogelio a stern warning to keep our conversation between the three of us and to stay out of trouble, we teleported back to Kit's apartment. Thane wasted no time filling in my best friend and partner in crime, who sat behind her desk in the corner of the living room, typing something into her computer.

"Okay, two more names for our list," he said.

I collapsed onto the couch, but my discomfort wasn't from the teleporting sickness. I wished it was, though.

Thane's eyebrows pulled together. "You shouldn't be feeling this bad now."

"It's not from the mode of travel," I said as I closed my eyes and rubbed my temples. "We can cross Xavier off the list."

That was the only good news to come from this disaster I found myself in. Xavier already had someone looking for the damn jewelry box—me. And I had failed.

"Why?" Thane asked.

"He's the buyer that hired me."

The sound of Kit typing ceased.

"You accepted a contract with the Master Vampire of Miami?" Thane asked, his tone incredulous.

"I didn't know he was the Master," I protested. "I didn't even know it was Xavier until just now."

"Girl, you're fucked." Kit wasn't one for sugarcoating anything.

I groaned. Served me right for being drawn to people who got right to the point. "I'll figure that out later. For now, we need to find the demon, hope he still has the soul and jewelry box, and clear my name."

My stomach couldn't handle dwelling on the fact that my life was basically forfeit if I didn't succeed. If Xavier caught me—which was highly likely now that I knew who he was—he might keep me alive. But I could only assume that a life enslaved to a Master Vampire wouldn't be a life at all.

What I did know, if nothing else, was that I needed to clear my reputation by proving my innocence before the week was over. I needed at least one win out of this whole clusterfuck before deciding who to give the damn box to.

My life was doomed either way.

If I had just protected Mad a little better, the way I was supposed to, none of this would be happening. I wouldn't have turned to this life. Hell, maybe I would have followed a different path three years ago if I had just done something simple like look closer into his death.

Letting out a sigh, I realized I hadn't even had a chance to delve into the truth of his death yet. What kind of a terrible sister was I?

"What do we know about the demon Mammon?" I asked, getting my mind back on track.

I wouldn't fail Mad again, but I also wouldn't be much help to him if I got caught by the DEA or Xavier. I continued to massage my temples, my head throbbing in tune with my heartbeat. The image sounded like beautiful music, but the notes were a hateful score.

"This Mammon is not one of the seven princes," Kit said, and the click-clack of her keyboard started up again. "He's one of the lower lackeys able to enter this world, which means he probably brought the items to his boss."

Gentle hands took my fingers off my head and set my palms across my chest. I would have said the new hands were unfamiliar, except the touch turned my skin molten. Thane's fingers rubbed at my temples, sending heat waves down to my toes. The throb started to dissipate with each soothing circle he made, and my belly started to flutter instead.

"Who does he work for?" I asked, trying to keep my thoughts focused on the job.

"Aamon," Kit said. "A Grand Marquis, still not very high up in the demon world, but high enough that he can't enter this plane of existence."

"Has he ever shown any desire for changing his status?" Thane asked. There was a pause, and then he asked in an almost bewildered voice, "What?"

With my eyes still closed, I imagined Kit had given him one of her infamous, "Are you stupid?" faces. I held back the giggle that wanted to escape. My headache was almost gone, so I brushed the reaper's hands away and sat up.

Thane moved to lean against the kitchen counter a few feet away.

"Most demons would give an arm or a leg, or more, to move up in the ranks or out," Kit explained.

The living room windows exploded into the apartment, and tiny glass shards burrowed into my arm as I raised it instinctively. A roar that set even my toes quivering followed less than a second later. When I lowered my arm, unable to feel the pain just yet, thanks to spiking adrenaline, a red-maned lion stood in Kit's apartment, almost within arm's reach from my seat on the couch.

Except it wasn't just a lion.

A long black scorpion tail complete with stinger arced up and over the beast's back, avoiding the massive wings folding down against his back. Thick, leathery membranes and pointed talons made the wings both weapons and armor at once. The face was vaguely reminiscent of a bearded man, but when he opened his mouth to roar again, several rows of razor-sharp teeth glistened in the light.

A motherfucking manticore.

How the hell had he found me here? Sure, they made for excellent trackers and often worked as beasts for hire, but Kit's wards should have shielded us better.

I rolled backward over the couch as he lifted his stinger to strike. Not a very graceful move, but a necessary one. The couch vibrated with each thud as the beast's stingers sank into the fabric. I had closed my eyes during the roll, and when I opened them, the stingers came out the couch's back.

I gulped. One hit from any of those poisoned blades, and I'd be dead.

"Veronica, come to me!" Kit yelled from her place behind her desk.

I chanced a glance around the right side of the couch. She had called up a fortified defensive shield to protect that entire corner of her apartment. To Kit, wards were more science than magic, and I just went along with whatever she said. Never question the genius.

Thane still leaned against the kitchen counter, utterly unperturbed by the creature. Few beings would attack a reaper unprovoked. If they did, the entire agency would be after them.

I dove out from behind the couch and instantly found myself pinned down by the manticore. His paws held my shoulders against the floor. I grimaced as his hot breath wafted onto my face. The smell of foul decay and rotting meat made my stomach churn in revolt. I held his head back with my arms as much as I could.

Pulling up my legs, I pushed my feet against his belly and rocked my hips up, throwing all my weight into the move. Surprise was on my side, and probably luck, too. The beast flipped over my head, and I leaped to my feet.

Thane raised his eyebrows at my display of strength. I was quickly ruining any secrecy I had left.

Another roar shook the entire apartment behind me, sending trinkets and glassware flying and shattering as they hit the ground. I ducked and dove toward Kit's barrier just as the manticore swiped at me. Its massive paw caught one of my feet, yanking my legs out from under me. I hit the tile floor hard. Stunned, I still had the smart idea to roll to the side. A boom rocked the room as the paw landed where my head had been only a breath before.

A sharp, burning sensation ripped through my shoulder. The manticore pinned me with one of his obsidian wing talons, buried all the way through my body to the tile beneath. Gritting my teeth against the pain, I managed to work free one of the knives I kept around my waist with my uninjured arm. I pushed fire into the blade and sliced up through the wing's membranes. The reek of singed flesh blew straight up my nose. Not the wisest move on my part, but the only one I could think of at the moment.

The manticore howled and pulled his wing free of my shoulder, dragging me up to my feet in the process. Not even waiting to regain my balance, I threw myself toward Kit, who caught me and pulled me behind her shield. I joined her in crouching on the far side of the desk.

The beast growled and turned his attention on Thane, lowering himself to pounce on new prey. His torn wing hung limply on the floor.

I held a hand to my shoulder as I turned to watch, trying not to think about how much my whole arm hurt and how much of my blood was getting everywhere. Witnessing an epic showdown between a reaper and anything else was beyond rare, and I was *not* going to miss it.

Thane finally pushed himself off the counter and approached the lion-like creature. His eyes turned a darker shade of blue, almost black, and seeped from his pupils to cover all the white.

"You would attack me?" The reaper's voice came out calm and even, but the threat behind his words dripped like acid, burning with each syllable.

The manticore paused, his ears twitching and turning to the side as if only now realizing what he faced.

"Who sent you?" Thane asked as he stalked toward the giant cat.

See, the thing about manticores is they never do anything on their own. They are purely beasts for hire, and most respectable Community members don't use their services. Bounty hunters aren't always respectable.

"I am forbidden from revealing my master," the manticore hissed back as he circled the reaper.

"Not from me," Thane said, reaching a hand into his pocket and pulling out the t-port device. Except when he pressed the button this time, a staff extended from either end of the cylinder, topped with a long, curved blade and wickedly sharp.

A scythe for The Reaper.

"That cat is fucked," Kit whispered beside me. I grinned in excited agreement.

As Thane approached, dark shadows billowed out around him. The manticore whined and lowered himself down to the ground, his ears flattened against his mane. The reaper reached the creature's head and stopped, setting the bottom of the staff beside the manticore's face, within eyesight.

"I'll ask once more, who sent you?"

"Aamon," the beast hissed.

Well, that confirmed it. If this Grand Marquis of a demon felt threatened enough to send a fucking manticore to stop us, we must be getting too close to the truth. I would have to cross my fingers and send a prayer to Dazhbog that the surface-dwelling demon, Mammon, still had the box.

Oh, and the soul, too, but I really, *really* needed that box back.

"Return to Aamon and let him know I will be paying a visit," Thane said in that same acidic voice that burned with each syllable. He turned to walk back toward the counter.

"You can tell him yourself," the manticore growled before raising his tail, aiming his stinger at the reaper's exposed back. "In hell."

CHAPTER 14

Sunday Afternoon

Thane, look out!" I yelled, leaping to my feet behind Kit's desk. Sharp pain blossomed in my shoulder as the wound pulled with my movement, and I immediately regretted making it. He could handle the beast; he was a reaper, for flames' sake.

The manticore let loose a volley of spikes from the end of his tail. Thane spun while raising his staff and knocked each spike from the air as if swatting away flies. As the last one fell, he pointed the blade at the beast and chanted, the words ancient and saturated with dark magic.

Death had come knocking.

The manticore tried to scramble away but found himself held in place by the reaper's magic, his massive paws scrabbling against the floor. A beam of bright white light arched out from the scythe's blade and enveloped the creature threatening the reaper.

"No, no!" the beast growled, still trying to resist the magic that pulled him closer to Thane. His lion-like body slid along the tile. "You cannot do this."

"Attacking with the intent to kill one of Death's own is a life forfeit," Thane intoned in a voice much deeper than usual. Black lines now wriggled out from around his darkened eyes and spread across his skin like an infection. He held out his free hand toward the manticore, palm facing up. As he chanted again, the beast's chest began to glow, a golden light swirling deep within his core.

The glow drifted up the manticore's throat and out his open, snarling mouth. An orb of light drifted lazily in the air toward Thane before resting in his free hand. The manticore let out a final sigh and collapsed lifeless onto the floor, loosed from the reaper's hold at last.

Judge, jury, and executioner.

I exchanged wide-eyed glances with Kit. Neither of us had seen a reaping before. A pang of sadness gripped my heart with the loss of the manticore, another nearly extinct species. But the fucker had tried to kill me and left me with a gaping hole in my shoulder, so my sorrow didn't last too long. I was a firm believer in the survival of the fittest.

Kit let down the shield and we both moved out from behind the desk, though we stayed back from Thane, who still had the creepy-black-eyes look going for him.

The reaper gazed intently at the orb of swirling golden light in his palm—the beast's soul—and pushed the button on the scythe. Both ends of the weapon retracted back into the smaller, cylindrical t-port device, which he tucked away in his pocket. I stood there with my mouth hanging open, not even trying to pretend I understood how magic made the giant curved blade fit inside.

He pulled out a small leather pouch dangling from a cord around his neck, small enough that it hadn't even created a bulge beneath his shirt. Or, you know, magic could have helped. He loosened the tie at the top and poured the soul inside like liquid gold. The black veins around his eyes retracted, and the whites of his eyes returned.

The adrenaline pounding through my veins started to die down, and fury rose in its place. Fury as I realized that a bounty hunter was able to track me down through all of Kit's defensive wards, and they had also put my best friend's life in danger. My body shook with anger. This situation was completely unacceptable.

"How the hell did it track me here?" I asked. "Did one of your wards fail?"

Kit shook her head. "Manticores are immune to elemental magic, and considering how close to extinction they are, I never would have expected an attack like this."

"I hate to reap and run, but I've got to take this," Thane patted the pouch around his neck, "and that," he nodded toward the manticore's body, "back to the agency. Get somewhere safer and try not to get attacked until I get back."

"How are you going to carry…" my voice trailed off as he bent down to the beast's limp form and hefted it over his shoulders like it weighed little more than a sack of potatoes.

My body tingled in all the right places as his hard muscles moved beneath tanned skin. And just like that, the desire was back.

Ay ay ay.

Kit's elbow in my side reminded me to shut my mouth. At least I hadn't drooled. I wiped my chin just to be sure.

Thane slipped his t-port device from his pocket again and was gone a second later.

Shaking her head, Kit opened a closet near her kitchen and pulled out some cloths, an elastic first-aid wrap, and a jar of something that looked like congealed vomit. "Never thought I'd see something like that in my lifetime."

When she opened the lid of the jar, it smelled like vomit, too.

"Me either," I said, eyeing her warily. "What *is* that?"

"A healing poultice made from various herbs. It works like a charm but without the magic," she explained as she poured the contents onto one of the cloths. Poured was too gentle a word—more like globbed.

"Please tell me you're not planning to put that anywhere near me." I backed away but didn't get far before a wall impeded my progress.

Kit gave me a look. "Don't be such a baby. Besides, you're still dripping on my floor."

She closed in and cornered me. I heaved a sigh and surrendered, removing my sticky hand from the front of my shoulder. Within seconds, she had the poultice-covered cloth expertly secured to my body with the elastic wrap. She'd had plenty of practice wrapping wounds during the war.

Satisfied with her work on me, Kit stepped with caution over broken glass to get to her coat closet and pulled out a broom and dustpan.

"Why don't you just wave your hand and whip this mess away?" I asked as she began to sweep up the broken glass. With her ability to tap into the earth element, pulling the natural materials in the glass together into a pile would be as easy for her as taking a deep breath.

"Using magic for mundane daily tasks makes people weak," she said quietly. The soft tinkling of glass hitting glass followed.

"I wouldn't call cleaning up a busted out living room window a mundane task." After that, I stopped arguing and washed the blood from my hands and arm. I helped pick up the things that had fallen over or broken during the explosion and subsequent fight. Thankfully, not a whole lot had. Maybe she kept her apartment somewhat bare for a reason.

During the cleanup, I noted with pleasure that the pain in my shoulder had subsided to just a nuisance. The medicine might have made me smell like a rotten swamp monster, but it did its job well.

"I want you to stay at my place," I said, as I mopped up my blood with a few towels. "My *real* place."

She gave me a face. "Only because I helped ward it."

After dumping the last collection into the trash, she tucked the broom and dustpan back into the closet. I would send a Community cleaning company to finish up. It was the least I could do, considering it was my blood staining her rug.

WHEN WE FINISHED setting up Kit in one of the penthouse guest rooms and ensuring she had everything she needed tech-wise—as far as I could provide, anyway—we settled onto the L-shaped couch in my living room to track down Mammon, the demon who caused this whole mess.

Kit did, at any rate. I had my own form of prep.

First, I went to a cabinet in my bathroom and pulled out a four-ounce glass bottle. I had purchased the potion from a witch when I started my acquisition gig and accidentally discovered the inherent dangers of my new job. I might have studied the Community species all my life, but it was another thing entirely to come face-to-face with an angry pixie.

After peeling off the poultice-soaked bandage and cleaning as much of the vomit-pulp as possible, I slathered the lotion-like contents from the bottle over the open wound. The hole had mostly stopped bleeding but stung like a sonofabitch when I touched it.

I hissed through my teeth as the magic took effect and stitched my skin together again. Good as new. When I was satisfied the healing was done, I peeled off my bloodstained clothes and pulled on new ones. I'd save the shower for after my meeting with the demon.

"He'll know you're coming," Kit said when I returned to the living room. She typed away on the laptop that she never left home without. Hidden among a wealth of stickers gracing the outside shell was a series of protection wards, keeping the device safe from physical harm and cyber-attacks of any kind. "The manticore would have returned to his boss by now if Thane hadn't reaped its soul."

The automatic lights in various rooms of the penthouse clicked on with the fading light. Actual sunset was still an hour or so away, but it had come far too quickly today. That's what happened when you've tracked down a couple of reapers, a witch and a warlock, and got attacked by a manticore. All in a day's work.

One by one, I took out the knives I kept hidden in various sized body sheaths and sharpened the blades. I laid the sheaths out on my coffee table while I determined which to wear for this hunt. Most were small throwing knives, easily hidden anywhere on my person with a single layer of clothing. Another handful were for a more direct form of combat. All had been specially branded to look like a fireball racing down the handle.

Good impressions called for good-looking weapons.

I might not have been a murderer, but I didn't have any problems with inflicting bodily harm. I'd only killed two people to this day, and their faces still haunted my nightmares every once in a while. Both kills happened the year after my parents returned to the sun, before I learned to control my rage.

I'd also since discovered new ways of bringing my opponents down, like coating the blades with a paralyzing poison. I just didn't have many opponents before now.

"Got him," Kit said, stirring me out of the trance-like state I often fell into when readying my blades. Cathartic, even.

My phone pinged with a message from Thane, asking me to let him know when and where to meet.

"Perfect timing," I said. "Where's the demon hiding?"

"He's set up 'home' at the South Florida Container Terminal," she said. A map flashed up on my phone, pinpointing one container in particular.

Time to find out what this demon was made of. Figuratively and likely literally.

CHAPTER 15

Sunday Evening

My Benz was still parked in the garage leading to the Shadow Market, so I messaged Thane with my car's location before suiting up. Besides the usual stash of hidden knives and guns, I also took the short sword I had nicknamed Lisa, because facing demons was the only time I took out the sword.

Like vampires, demons could be killed by decapitation, but they were much harder to catch. Unlike the bloodsuckers who were once mere humans, spawns of hell could use magic just as well as any well-trained witch or mage. The only "good" thing about demons was the fact that they didn't spend a whole lot of time in the human realm because their magic drained fast aboveground and didn't replenish quickly.

Kit had given me the weirdest look when she first met Lisa, but then I explained the name meant she-fox in Russian, the human language based on phoenix lore from days of old. Sneaky like a fox, no one expected that this wee blade could do the damage she did in the right hands—like mine.

Technically, demons weren't a part of the Community, but the DEA still frowned on unnecessary killings. I would say self-defense counted as a necessary killing, which was why I didn't include them in the number of people I had killed. They weren't people, and they had a nasty habit of showing up during my contracts.

Anyway, I didn't mean to neglect Lisa so much, but I preferred knives and guns for my regular jobs, both of which were easier to hide on busy Miami streets. In reality, cutting through obstacles with any blade wasn't so difficult once I imbued the steel with my inner fire. Demon bones and muscles were nothing compared to that heat, but I liked to take Lisa for a spin every once in a while to keep her running smoothly.

After a quick flight over to the garage, I landed on the roof of a truck parked near my Benz. The reaper had beaten me there with his t-port device, no big surprise. He sighed and leaned against the passenger side of my bright red car, checking the time on his watch. I was sure it was some standard-issue reaper smartwatch, but from here, it just looked like a regular, old-fashioned analog.

Sun and flames, the man was hot. I felt like a broken record or a sex-driven teen with how often I noticed his appearance, but it was like death had enhanced his already-beautifully-defined features. Even in my current falcon form, my pulse quickened as I imagined what it would feel like to have him push me up against the parking garage wall. I'd wrap my legs around his waist, and—

Shit. I needed to stop that line of thought. Although priority number one after this mess was all cleaned up was to get laid and not with a fucking reaper. I could do better than that. Maybe not in looks, but, you know, alive.

I hopped to the ground behind the truck and shifted into my human shape. After smoothing my ponytail back, then chiding myself for doing so, I stepped around the truck and headed toward Thane.

He looked up as I approached, his eyes narrowing. "I didn't sense your approach. Did you fly in?"

"Didn't your momma teach you it's rude to touch other people's things?" I pressed the button on my key fob to remote start the vehicle and smiled as the Benz roared to life.

Thane didn't even blink. Damn it. Making him jump could have been a fun moment. What would it take to spook a reaper?

"Get in," I said as I slid into the driver's seat. I reached back and placed the sheath holding Lisa on the backseat. "Demons can sense magic used nearby, so we can't use your travel method. Besides, it's a nice evening."

He opened the door and sat on the seat next to me. "You didn't answer my question."

"You're very observant." I backed the luxury sedan out of the parking spot and followed the exit signs out of the garage.

"What's with the sword?" he asked.

"Lisa."

"Excuse me?"

"The sword's name is Lisa," I explained, "and she goes demon hunting with me."

"Should I understand some joke in there?"

"Not unless you speak Russian." I laughed as he let out an exasperated breath.

We drove in silence for a while after that, me trying to enjoy the setting sun's fading rays painting everything in hues of pinks and purples while avoiding thinking of the delicious heat radiating off the man next to me.

I shook my head. Not a man—a dead man. A reaper. Yes, I needed to focus on that fact. But it was weird that he would be emitting heat instead of the cold of death. Even Sophia had a chill about her, but maybe that was just her personality.

Speaking of the cold of death…

"So, how'd you die?" I asked as if asking how his day went. I took the next turn.

Thane ran a hand through his hair in an almost embarrassed gesture. "Overdose."

Ah. That suited the little bit I knew of him. Not a junkie, I'd wager, nor a suicide like I thought Mad did; a party boy. "And that's how you turned up grim?"

He smirked. "I suppose I liked to party a bit too much to earn wings right after death."

Bingo. "Is that why you were at the mansion with Sophia?"

He glanced at me. "You know Sophia?"

Oops. "We met once, totally randomly... Are you two together?" Double oops. I pursed my lips. Why did my brain have to go in *that* direction with my distracting question? I didn't want to know because I didn't want to think of him in a romantic kind of way. If he was into Sophia, more power to them. Mazel tov to the happy couple.

"Together? Like dating?" he asked. "Reapers don't exactly date."

"But she wants to, right? She laid her claim on you pretty clearly that night." Her fierce look of possession when we ran into each other at the mansion hadn't been hard to read. And there I went asking another question I didn't really want to be answered. I wanted to smack myself.

Was I jealous? Of Sophia?

I almost snorted out loud at the absurdity. I had lived twenty-seven years without caring too much about the men who came in and out of my life, hating that I had been reminded for eighteen years how important it was that I continue the phoenix species as soon as possible.

Seeing men as a means just for breeding kind of took the fun out of dating. I wasn't about to start caring now about some dead guy who couldn't physically provide what I needed—what my *species* required, at any rate.

"We don't always get what we want."

I glanced at him, feeling like he had just read my mind before I remembered asking him about Sophia. Better to keep my mouth shut at this point. We fell into another silence. Well, we would have if I hadn't been so terrible at awkward silences.

"So, how long have you been a reaper?" I asked after only a minute or two. Might have been more like thirty seconds.

"A few years."

I rolled my eyes. A few years could mean three or three hundred to his kind. Earning wings could be quick, or it could last a dozen human lifetimes. Failing to receive a pair meant burning for all eternity, I just didn't know exactly how long that took or how they decided it was time.

"How much longer do you have?" I asked, trying a new angle.

Thane shrugged and turned his gaze on me. "Are you going to confirm my suspicion that you're one of the rare avian shifters? Or tell me how you caught Rogelio's fireball and then ate it?"

"Some things are better off a mystery," I said. Through the dusk, a rainbow of colors making up the Tetris-like shipping yard appeared in front of us. "We're here."

I parked the Benz in one of the parking lots for the cruise ship terminals and reattached the belt sheath holding Lisa. Everything was closed for the evening, so we'd need to let ourselves in. After double-checking the location of the container in question, I picked the gate's lock, and we headed into the shipping yard.

The closer we got, the more my skin tingled in anticipation. My nose even itched, making me rub it every few steps. We'd kick this demon's ass—well, I would. Thane had made it clear he couldn't interfere unless he was attacked directly like with the manticore.

But after said ass kicking, Thane would reap the stolen soul, I would give the box to Xavier, I would be cleared of a murder, and I wouldn't become Xavier's next sex slave or meal. Not too much to ask. I would have to pray to every god and goddess I could think of that Xavier wouldn't destroy the world or something like that with whatever the box did. I was reasonably sure I'd have found out if it was capable of such destruction.

I unsheathed Lisa and a smaller knife, ready for anything. The demon had to know we were coming for him; I just hoped to have the upper hand with surprise on the when.

Light came from under the door of the metal container we sought, the rusting metal opening standing slightly ajar. A low voice spoke on the other side, but I couldn't tell if he was muttering to himself or to someone else. I crept closer until I was able to peek through the crack at the jamb.

A demon dressed in a man's skin sat on an overturned crate, holding a cell phone out in front of him. The human body that he mimicked had shaggy blond hair down to his chin, a scruff-covered chin, and blue eyes. Along with the killer tan and flip flops, he could easily drop everything and go shred the gnar at any moment.

If I hadn't known that he was really a wolf in sheep's clothing—or a demon in human skin in this case—I might have even found the guy attractive. Yuck.

Once I had learned the signs to look for, telling a demon from a human happened in one glance. Unless they got lucky like this one did, the skin would either be stretched too tight across the demon's form or hang loose.

He stopped muttering and tilted his head as if listening to something. I held my breath, but I feared the pounding of my heart would give me away. It sure drowned out my hearing. But the demon shook his head at the phone screen and continued to mutter.

I let out my breath slowly, counting to ten. I needed to go in with as much confidence and nerves of steel as I could muster.

The main problem with demons—besides the obvious, of course—is that they had no scruples with anything. He could dismember me and eat my heart for breakfast without ever thinking he'd done anything even remotely wrong. Breakfast is breakfast.

After he ended the call and hurled his phone into a pile of packing paper, I made my move.

"This is home sweet home, huh?" I said as I stepped around the door.

He leaped to his feet with a growl, his eyes glowing red—another handy way to tell if someone were really a demon. I smiled. Surprise had worked in my favor. I wanted him off guard and not thinking straight.

"Let's make this quick: you give me the box and the soul, and I let you live," I said. "Deal?"

I knew it wouldn't be that easy, but it was always worth a shot to play nice.

With a howl, he lunged toward me. His nails extended into claws which were intended to rake through flesh as easily as through paper. I deflected his attack with my sword while bringing my knife up and earning myself a roar of pain. Black liquid dripped from the slash in his thigh onto the shipping container's floor.

Blood the color of an oil spill was a tricky—and sometimes fatal—way to spot a demon, but impossible to argue against. The paralyzing poison slicked onto my blades didn't work well against his type, but it would slow him down.

He looked from the slash on his leg to me with fury written on his face. Poor guy. He still didn't know who he faced. Snarling, he chanted and cast a spell in my direction. It was probably something to chain me or end me, but I dove to the side. The spell crashed into a metal wall with a resounding clang and sparks as I rolled back onto my feet.

I swung Lisa at his neck. The hit wouldn't decapitate him in one go, but it would hurt like a sonofabitch and give me the upper hand. He raised an arm instead, allowing the steel to sink into the bone. With a deep growl, he pulled his arm toward him, which dragged me along with it. He swung at me with his other fist. I ducked, wrenching Lisa free with a twist.

"You seriously can't help this go faster?" I asked Thane as I deflected another attack. I kicked the demon in his chest, sending him backward onto his butt.

"You're doing just fine," Thane said from his place leaning against the door.

I rolled my eyes, shifted into the falcon, and dove toward the demon. I slashed at his eyes as I swooped over his head. Flesh and muscle ripped beneath my talons. I landed behind him and shifted back into a human crouch with Lisa held out in front of me.

While he held his hands to his face to stop the blood flowing from his ruined eyes, I swept my leg out, kicking his feet out from under him. I rolled away as he crashed to the ground. Before he could stand again, I was on top of him. After dropping my knife, I pinned his arms by his sides with my knees and his legs with my feet. I held Lisa to his throat with both hands, ready to heat the metal and push through to the floor.

"The box and soul. Now." I bore down on the blade, letting black liquid form beneath the metal.

"I don't have them," he said, his snarl turning into a bemused smile.

"If only I believed that," I said with a tsk-tsk.

"You don't have to believe it, but I'm in as deep a shit-filled pit as you are." His blue eyes, now partially healed as the skin and muscle stitched themselves back together, widened as he looked at something behind me. "I swear! Check my phone."

I chanced a glance over my shoulder to spot Thane approaching. "Oh, good, you're finally helping. Can you do the honors?"

The reaper reached through the mess of papers to the phone, then looked at the demon in question.

"Text message from the boss," Mammon said, gulping even though it caused more ink-colored blood to flow from beneath my blade. His boss might have been in hell, but that didn't stop him from using modern technology. The phone bill must have been a doozy.

Thane read me the message, "My winged lion comes for you next. Find the items I seek."

Fuck my life. He spoke the truth.

I didn't understand. Everything pointed to Mammon. According to Rogelio, only Xavier and the demon had enough power to take a soul, besides the reapers and a handful of witches, of course. So either Rogelio was lying, or he didn't know someone else who had that much power. Maybe it wasn't even someone in Miami. Because if it wasn't the demon, that left Xavier, which didn't make much sense.

Why would he have hired me to steal the box if he had someone else do it first?

Unless…

Shivers skittered up my spine and gripped my throat, making it hard to breathe.

I tumbled off the demon and scooted backward on my butt, gasping for breath. Lisa clattered to the metal floor by my side. My vision went hazy, and I was vaguely aware of the demon running out of the shipping container. It didn't matter—it hadn't been him.

Thane's face appeared in front of me, crouching, his eyebrows pulled together. "What just happened?"

I took a deep, shuddering breath before I could respond.

"Xavier set me up."

CHAPTER 16

Sunday Evening

W hy would Xavier set you up?" Thane asked.

Any number of reasons passed through my mind, my body trembling. To be his slave, his next meal, his trophy. The list could go on. Xavier was a Master Vampire, the head of the Miami court. How I hadn't connected the dots to his identity long ago was beyond me. I had gotten sloppy, and my sloppiness might have caused my ruin.

My parents had warned me against this life and taught me to live one of protection and defense, staying invisible as much as possible. But the only other person I had intended to protect was gone, taken from me, and I still had no idea how or why. I pressed the heels of my hands to my eyes, as if that could somehow lessen the pain of losing him.

Becoming a thief might have fallen into my lap by chance, but if I was honest with myself, I relished the idea of breaking free from the mold my parents had created.

With Mad's death, I told myself I wasn't capable of protecting anyone. So, I went the opposite way as soon as the opportunity arose. I embraced the dance with danger that each contract gave me—the thrill of the hunt, the chase, the glory. More than once, I saw my death dance before my eyes only to escape on a wing and a prayer—figuratively and literally.

I should have died dozens of times by now, even if I could be reborn. No one else knew that I was a phoenix besides Kit, the angels, and whichever level of reaper now had access to the classified part of my file.

All Xavier knew was my reputation and skill level. He knew I could shift forms, and if he had done thorough homework before hiring me, which I was sure he had, he knew I had a little magic up my sleeve. I was good at hiding it, but a few extreme situations had required I use it. The mystery of what I was must have drawn his attention, and now my life was unraveling before me.

It had been easy to look past the truth staring me in the eye because that truth meant accepting my faults. Who the hell wanted to do that?

"Fuck!" I yelled instead of answering Thane. Sometimes it felt good to shout out a good old-fashioned swear word.

The reaper raised his eyebrows and stood from his crouch, holding out a hand to help me to my feet. After sheathing my knife and grabbing my sword, I took his hand, allowing the heat of his touch to wash out the terror that had started to creep in.

"Why do you think it's Xavier?" he asked as we left the container and headed back to my car. We could leave in different ways, but I didn't want to leave my car there, and Thane seemed glued to my side at the moment. I didn't know if I liked or hated that thought. Right now, it felt like a bit of both.

"I don't just think it, I know it." I held up a hand. "And no, I'm not explaining."

He sighed. "You know, I may be able to help if you let me in a little."

"I thought you were just going to tag along, not involve yourself too much." My tone was getting snippy.

"That was before I truly believed you were innocent."

"Oh, just now, huh? I didn't realize the agency hired liars," I said, letting my anger at being played by Xavier get the best of me. I wasn't some mouse, some prey to be teased.

"I may like to party, but I don't do pity parties," Thane said as he pulled out his t-port device, the lines of his cheeks moving as he clenched his jaw. "Let me know when you've put your big girl pants back on."

And with that, he was gone.

I mimicked him in the air, flailing my hands around like I was some big bad reaper. I knew I looked ridiculous, but somehow the humor of it made me feel better.

Of course he was right, but I was far from the mood to admit it.

AN HOUR LATER, I parked the Benz in my favorite nondescript garage near the Brickell Flatiron. Normally, I would wing straight back to my penthouse sanctuary, shower, eat, and get some much-needed sleep.

But tonight I needed to stomp off some steam against the sidewalks, mad at my utter lack of judgment and sloppiness with this job. I left Lisa tucked under a towel in the backseat of the Benz, not wanting to draw any attention by parading around at night with a sword on my hip.

Others might have considered a walk careless, but others weren't me. Not only was I more than capable of handling myself in a fight in human form, but I could also shift into a bird and fly away if I needed to. Only Kit knew about my penthouse apartment here at the Flatiron, and I had made sure no one followed me before I parked in the garage.

I tucked my hands into my pockets as I strode down the street, trying hard to curb my resting bitch face.

Okay, I was slowly admitting to myself that I had become more and more reckless since my parents died. I had to be, to miss the signs with my brother's death. If I had been what my parents expected me to be, he might still be alive. Mad didn't come back to life—as a phoenix should do outside of a true death—because he hadn't gone through the rebirth ceremony yet. At sixteen, he was two years away from it. What a dumb tradition.

And now, because I still hadn't learned from all my previous mistakes, my life was on the line in a way it had never been before.

I heaved a sigh. Xavier had the jewelry box, which meant it was impossible to fulfill his contract, a fact he would never accept. Sure, I could live life on the run, if living was even what you would call it. Running from town to town, country to country, avoiding every major city to hide from the vampires. I would be looking over my shoulder for the next five hundred years or so.

But was that my only other option?

If so, that also meant that the phoenix species would die with me. There was no way I could pop out a few babies and raise a family with vampires hunting me down. I had avoided the topic of procreation for way too long, and now I might not even have the option anymore.

I kicked a pebble off the sidewalk, wishing with everything inside me that I could have another chance. Wishing I had made smarter decisions. Wishing I hadn't been such a motherfucking moron.

It wasn't until I was a few feet past an alley that I realized I was being followed. I sighed. Speaking of morons…

I turned on my heel fast, a knife in hand ready to throw, only to find nothing and no one. I scanned the streets, hawk-like vision narrowing to see farther than a human while also picking up heat signatures—still nothing. But the hairs on the back of my neck wouldn't lie back down, and my stomach clenched with unease.

I backtracked to the alley and glanced down it. Like I said, I wasn't some prey to be toyed with. I would face my attacker head-on. Bodily reactions to fear were nothing more than necessary instinct survival skills, alerting me to a potential threat. I embraced them because, without them, I would have been dead many times over.

The alley was empty, all the way through to the opposite end where it opened up on the next street. Devoid of humans and Community members anyway. Rats and cockroaches were busy dumpster-diving in the smorgasbord behind every big city restaurant. Brick walls enclosed the passage, allowing approximately three meters of space between. A streetlight a few feet away barely lit the opening on this side. The rest of the narrow road leading from one end of the building to the other was dark.

Keeping my knife out and ready, though held in a way to keep it hidden against my forearm, I strolled down the alley. I feigned nonchalance while I sought my follower as well as any additional weapons I might be able to use depending on what new threat I faced. Broken bottles, well-used furniture, and a few hefty bags of trash might come in handy.

An odd knowing sensation slithered down my spine, turning my blood to ice and halting my stride. I looked up and immediately wished I hadn't. My heart thudded hard against my chest. But not seeing wouldn't have been any better.

In the near pitch-black of the pathway, they crawled down the walls on either side, headfirst, their clawed hands gripping the bricks like a lizard's. Eyes the deep red shade of imminent death bored into mine.

Vampires.

Xavier was coming to collect, and this time, I was all alone.

CHAPTER 17

Sunday Night

Six vampires made it down the walls and raised themselves to stand hunched over before me. Six was only half a brood, which meant the other half was most likely up on the roofs, watching and waiting—the bloodsuckers always traveled in a brood.

Like predators on a hunt, they spread out around me, a few giggling as they stared at me with unrestrained lust. Not the giggle of a happy child, but of a hungry hyena about to feast.

The fact that Xavier sent a brood confirmed that the Master Vampire knew I was more than I seemed. At least it wasn't an entire nest. Despite my sweating palms, I smiled.

That must have spooked some of the newly created, because they stopped giggling. Silence filled the alley.

"Are we going to do this or what?" I asked, holding up my knife. Such a shame they hadn't faced me in the garage. Then they could have met Lisa.

The vampire in front hissed, exposing its extended canines. I assumed it was a he, but you never really knew with the younger ones. Newer vampires were humanoid because they were once human, but whatever made humans humane had long since shriveled up inside the creatures that stood before me. Presumably because they had to claw themselves out of their own coffins and graves through six feet of dirt and worms to claim their immortal birthright.

My nose crinkled in disgust as I let my gaze wander over its once-human form. Much like demons, vampire skin never seemed to fit their skeletons properly. At least not for a few centuries, when they finally started to pass for humans again. Until then, they were gangly, all arms and legs like a kid who just went through a growth spurt.

"The Master does not wish us to kill you," the vampire said. It didn't speak with a lisp, so it'd had plenty of years to grow accustomed to speaking through sharp, elongated teeth.

When it came to vampires, "newly created" and allowed to traipse above or below city streets meant several decades deceased, up to a century. However, they were not permitted to show their grotesque faces to humans. Not unless they were feeding, which became a whole other set of rules established by the DEA to follow.

"The feeling is not mutual," I said with a shrug.

The vampire narrowed its eyes. "However, he has authorized us to encourage your cooperation in whatever way we must."

I tapped the blade of my knife against my chin as if in thought. "I'm not feeling much like cooperating right now. It's been a hell of a day."

"Perhaps you require some motivation." The vampire raised a hand and crooked a still-shriveled and bony finger, not quite filled out properly yet.

A scuffle came from behind the creature before a man was thrust to his knees beside the vampire, a bag over his head and clawed hands holding him down. When the bag came off, it revealed a bound and gagged Rogelio. The warlock's eyes opened wide when he saw me.

I wasn't usually okay with someone being used to make me comply, but things were also starting to click into place, including one of the tattoos I saw on the warlock's neck earlier in the day. My nerves began to settle, only to be replaced by a slight tremor as my anger rose.

"I'm not sure why you expect me to care about this man," I said, tilting my head to the side.

Rogelio's eyes nearly bugged out of his head, filled with fear at my nonchalant response. He tried to get to his feet, but the hands on his shoulders pressed him down.

"You would let him die for your pride?" the vampire asked, the slightest hint of surprise in its voice.

"Two things." I held up two fingers like the vampire was too stupid to count. "One, I'm not a fucking hero."

I met Rogelio's watering eyes. "Two, even if I was a fucking hero, I wouldn't save a man marked for death." My gaze moved to one of the tattoos on his neck. Except I had finally realized it wasn't a tattoo.

The vampire followed my look before smiling. *El beso del diablo,* as it was called here in the Miami Community, was a mark given by the Master Vampire to those who sought immortality via vampirism. Just like reapers had to earn their wings, vampire wannabes had to prove themselves worthy of the real kiss, known as the kiss of death. Except it wasn't really a kiss so much as a bite which ended their lives and forced them to rise from the grave.

Those found unworthy would be sealed away in a coffin—alive. Having endured since ancient times, the barbaric ritual of rising from the grave was seen as a time-honored tradition. Noble, even. Yuck.

Unlike the Risen, those nearly mindless creatures created by necromancers—and a totally illegal practice these days, I might add—vampires were the result of a viral infection enhanced with magic. The infected blood first killed the host then reanimated its corpse several days, sometimes weeks, later.

The first kiss given to a candidate by a Master, *el beso del diablo*, left a burning brand upon the skin due to a reaction with the virus. It was usually placed in a spot hidden from the general populace. Xavier had left me a billboard-sized hint with his mark across Rogelio's carotid artery, where a significant amount of blood flowed. And I had missed it.

If I survived after this mess, I would take this job a whole lot more seriously—or be done with it altogether.

"Ah, Master has chosen well with you," the vampire said with an approving grin. "Shall we sweeten the stakes?" It paused for a moment before laughing, a grating and rasping sound that made me cringe. "No pun intended, of course."

After untying the top of a dark bag attached to a belt around its waist, the vampire reached a hand inside and withdrew a swirling golden orb of light—a soul. But I knew as well as he did that this wasn't just any soul. It was *the* soul. The one stolen from Broderick and the one I had been blamed for stealing.

Blamed was too kind a word. Let's try *falsely incriminated.*

I narrowed my eyes at the vampire. "I'm going to need that back."

"I thought as much." The creature nodded. "Come with me, without a fight, and this soul shall be returned to the agency."

I let out a sharp laugh. "I'll pass. Trusting the word of a vampire has never been high on my list of priorities. Xavier promised me a week to sort things out and look where that got me."

The vampire poured the soul back into the bag as if the light was actually a liquid. "As you wish."

That must have been the key phrase the others were all waiting for because a second later, the vampires attacked.

Now, I was far from humble when it came to my fighting skills—I had trained my entire life and earned the right to boast. But taking on six foes at once was a lot even for me. Add in the fact that it was six vampires trained to maim, drain, and kill, with six more watching up above, ready to take their places when they fell, and I was well and truly outnumbered.

But none of them had what I had—a tarnished reputation and a whole lot of anger issues.

Trying to hide a tremble born of equal parts fury and fear, I gripped the knife in my fist as they came at me. Shifting to escape was out of the question now that I knew they had the soul. If I had any hope of clearing my name, I couldn't leave without it.

So, I did the next best thing. I dove to the side while throwing my knife like my life depended on it.

Because it did.

A broken dining room chair leaned against the side of a dumpster, which I had noted before the vampires showed themselves. I tumbled over to it now, breaking off two wooden spindles that made up the backrest. Makeshift stakes weren't as effective as whittled ones or wooden crossbow bolts, but they would have to do.

The first vamp was easy to kill, but I just got lucky. It was a newly created who practically fell heart-first onto my stake in its bloodlust. The vamp's ribs crunched and gave way beneath the wood. Reanimation magic fled fast when vamps were staked, decapitated, or caught on fire. Their bodies crumpled into dust and brittle bones. The second and third circled me warily while the fourth and fifth took turns throwing themselves at me.

I ducked and thrust, earning snarls and hisses as my stake met flesh time and time again, just not in the right places. I dispatched another one with a well-aimed throw to the heart, but it also meant I lost one of my stakes. The vamps slowed as they circled me, warily assessing me with their glowing red eyes.

The older vampire who did all the talking took a few steps backward, the movement catching my eye. The bag at its waist did at any rate. That was all I really needed to grab, and then I could get the hell out of there. Using my inner fire would be the last resort because magic wasn't infinite, and I had to ensure I had enough up my sleeve to flee if it came to it.

I kicked the nearest vamp hard in the chest, sending it flying against one of the others. Another one lunged at me, and I jumped. The moment I was airborne, I shifted and dove for the older vamp, readying my talons to snatch and tear.

Something pulled at my throat, and I tumbled to the ground, the impact forcing me to shift back to my human form. A thin wire like a garrote pulled tight across my neck, the other end of the weapon held by the vampire with the bag. Fear sliced through my heart like an ice pick, feeling very much like caught prey.

I grasped at the metal wire enclosing around my throat, using my magic to heat it enough to slip through. Forget the bag, I needed to go. Now. This was too much for one to handle, no matter how pissed I was.

Before I could leap to my feet, multiple sets of hands grabbed and held me in place, claws digging painfully into my skin. On my knees, I struggled against the inhuman hands, but the unholy creatures had me. Fingers dug through my hair to my scalp before gripping it all in a fist and pulling my head back, exposing my neck.

The vampire in charge strode up to me, glaring down with flames for eyes. "Petulant child. I tried to make this painless for you. Now you have forced my hand."

"We both knew a fight was inevitable." I grimaced as the fist gripped my hair tighter, as if I were being scalped with a bare hand.

"The Master did not forbid us from feeding on you, nor draining you close to death. It will be easier to transport you drained, without waiting for your next attempt to flee." The vampire bared its fangs in a snarl and grabbed my shoulder in one hand. It pushed my head to the side with the other, fully exposing my pulsing arteries.

"And I look forward to tasting whatever it is that you are."

CHAPTER 18

Sunday Night

The vampire's raunchy breath blew across my throat, goosebumps racing down my back as the tiny hairs there moved. I swallowed hard, acutely aware of how visible the movement and sound would be to the bloodsuckers holding me.

From behind the vampire, a deep and delightfully familiar voice said, "I wouldn't, if I were you."

The vampires let go of my arms, and I scrambled back to my feet, brushing alley grit off my slim cargo pants. The vamps all skittered away, hissing as if the light emitting from Thane burned their eyes. Even I raised an arm to block out his intense rays, unable to see his entire form while he radiated like the sun.

Unlike legend had us believe, vampires didn't dissipate in the light of day. Direct sunlight made them rot several times faster than usual, which meant it took a lot more blood to recover from a day, or even a few hours, in the sun. They would all need to feed after this encounter with the reaper's holy light, a handy ability they only used against the undead.

"Reapers do not interfere in our affairs," hissed the older vampire who had been about to suck my blood.

"No, but I believe you have something that does not belong to you," Thane said, holding out a hand as he approached. "Return the soul."

The vampire's eyes darted around the alley and up to the rooftop. Only four remained on the ground, but I knew six more waited up top. I opened my mouth to warn the reaper.

"The rest of your brood has returned to the nest, as will you once you give me the soul," Thane continued before I could speak.

As the reaper got closer, the vampire in charge cringed away, steam rising from its skin as the light emitting from Thane washed over it.

"The Master will kill you for this," snarled the vampire as it removed the bag from its belt and held it out.

Thane accepted the bag and met the creature's gaze straight on.

The vampire's eyes burst into flames. Falling to its knees, it held its hands to its melting face, its screams making my blood run cold.

"He's welcome to try," the reaper said.

Saved by the burn.

Corny, I know. But in all seriousness, twice now, this reaper guy did little more than exist and managed to vanquish some major threats. No wonder the Community feared the agency as much as they did. Maybe I should start fearing them, too.

"Thanks," I said with a grin, squinting against his light. Or maybe I'd start being afraid another day.

The remaining vampires fled, including the one who would need to regrow its eyeballs. At least it could regrow them, right?

"Did you follow me?" I asked. While I wasn't a huge fan of the idea, he had certainly proved himself useful.

"No, you made it clear you needed some space," he said, looking me in the eye with a hint of humor. The light around him faded, and I blinked, trying to clear the circles that still stained my retinas. "He took the soul out of this bag, which is like a signal fire to my kind."

"That's helpful. So, time to get that back to the agency?" I asked with a pointed look at the bag in his hand.

"Not yet."

Thane untied the bag and withdrew the soul, letting the empty container drop to the ground. I guess he had his own fancy, agency-issued soulbag and didn't need a dirty vamp's. Who knew where the other one had been? I shuddered to think.

After setting the shimmering soul on the alley's paved ground as if it were made of super-thin glass, he held a palm over it and chanted. His eyes bled black as magic swirled around him, drawing the shadows closer. A warm breeze whipped through the narrow passage, stirring loose papers and plastic into a flurry.

The orb of light grew bigger, following Thane's hand as he raised it, until it stretched taller than the average man. Then its shape took on that of a person. Make that a fae man—the victim, Broderick. He was younger than I had imagined he would be, but then again, the fae didn't age like humans. Hundreds of years passed for them in the blink of a human eye.

Long, honey-brown hair hung straight down to his shoulders, and the tips of his pointed ears poked through. A white robe tied with a knotted cord clothed his body. The soul's entire being shimmered like he wasn't all there. After blinking his dark brown eyes a few times, his gaze settled on Thane. He bowed before the reaper.

"My apologies for disturbing your rest," Thane said.

"No apologies necessary, Soul Reaper." The fae dipped his head in a show of respect. "How can I assist you?"

"You and your killer were after a jewelry box hidden in a safe in Dr. Renauldo's home," Thane explained. "Do you know where the box is now?"

I did a double-take, staring open-mouthed at Thane. I knew he wanted the box at the end of all this, but why in Dazhbog's name wasn't he asking about the actual killer? "Hey, I think—"

Thane cut me off with a sharp glance.

"Once placed into the soulbag, I ceased to see, hear, or even think," the duke said, sadness in his tone.

I would bet the emotion came more from his own death than unable to answer the question. He didn't strike me as overly righteous, considering he had attempted to steal a powerful object to unseat his queen. Even if the queen was a fae supremacist.

See why I didn't follow fae politics? The lines were too blurry.

"Did you see your killer?" Thane asked, his voice calm though his jaw was clenched tight.

"I—" Broderick paused, his form glitching like a poor-quality video feed. "Something is happening. I can feel my soul called away."

Thane frowned. "Called away by whom?"

The fae's face took on a look of absolute horror, his lower lip trembling. His form began to fold and shrink backward, like he was being pulled somewhere. "Reap my soul before it is too late."

"Too late for what?" the reaper asked, but we both knew there was no more time for questions.

He chanted again, his eyes pooling with darkness. After a final bow to the fae's soul, he blew the man a kiss. Shadowy wisps swirled away from Thane's lips and toward the waiting soul.

Unlike a Master Vampire's that kept souls grounded to the earth, the Reaper's Kiss allowed souls to move on, wherever it was they were supposed to go. As the spectral of magic reached him, Broderick let out a sigh of relief. His shimmering form dissipated into thin air, swirling upward toward the sky.

Looked like he was going to the good place. Lucky him.

"Good luck, Soul Reaper," the fae's voice whispered in the air. "Don't trust…"

Then he was gone.

I blinked at Thane. "Well, that's fairly annoying."

"Fairly?" The corners of his lips quirked up, though his eyes remained deep in another train of thought.

"I'm being nice, of course." I bit my lip, chewing on it slightly. "So, you going to let the agency know I'm not responsible?"

He let out a sigh and ran a hand through his hair. "Yeah, but you're going to need to come with me this time."

Like the world was being deprived of its oxygen, a tightening of the air was the only warning we had before we found ourselves surrounded. The Death Enforcement Agency had arrived en masse via teleportation with various weapons held up and aimed straight at us.

I threw my hands up. "I didn't do it."

The tapping of heels against pavement came from behind me a moment before Sophia Clark stepped into view. Her piercing green eyes fixated on me, hurt shining in their depths. "To think I almost helped you. I should have known you'd sink your talons into one of our own."

I opened my mouth to protest, only I had no idea what she meant. "Wait, what?"

"Not only did you kill Broderick Ó Faoláin and steal his soul, you somehow convinced Thane to assist you." Sophia gave a cluck of her tongue. "That's low, even for you."

"Stop with the vague accusations," Thane said before I could word vomit obscenities all over her. "Veronica Neill is not responsible for Broderick's death."

"You acted alone?" Sophia asked, her eyes wide as she turned to face him directly.

"Not only did I not kill him, but you know that for a fact." Thane's eyes narrowed dangerously.

"I don't, actually. You had a chance to get to know this vile creature when I turned my back for a mere second." She tilted her head in my direction. "Who knows what else you were capable of doing that night."

"Don't be absurd," he said.

"We all know how motivated you are to earn your wings," Sophia said, disgust tainting her words. "I just never figured you to stoop this low, killing innocents ahead of time to reap their souls and increase your count."

Thane jerked his head back as if slapped, his eyes opened wide. "I would never—"

Sophia cut him off, "Thane Munro and Veronica Neill, you're both under arrest for the murder and soul theft of Broderick Ó Faoláin."

CHAPTER 19

Sunday Night

W hat gives you the right to arrest *me?*" Thane asked, his tone incredulous.

I was right there with him on the being baffled front. Things were happening way too fast for my brain to keep up.

"I do," a new voice added to the mix.

A man who might have been early retirement age, though maintaining thick sand-colored hair, stepped out of the shadows. His bright blue eyes shone with knowledge far beyond his years. Beyond this realm, even. He was roughly the same height as me but built like a linebacker—a lean, mean fighting machine. Like Thane, he wore crisp dress slacks below a button-down shirt, the sleeves rolled up to his elbows.

Thane immediately dropped to one knee and lowered his head. "Sir, there has been an error. May I explain?"

"I was wrong about you," the man said, his eyes both sharp and sad as he gazed at Thane's bowed head. "Bring him back to the agency. Both of them." He made a round-up gesture with his hand, a gem-embellished ring flashing on one of his fingers.

Thane snapped his head up and met my gaze before giving a quick tilt of his head. I took that as my cue to get the fuck out of there.

"Regretfully, I must decline the invitation," I said with a tiny curtsy before I shifted forms.

Diving between the line of reapers, I didn't seek height just yet. They fired at me, as expected. The whoosh of a net soared past me and collapsed around another reaper. His yell of surprise came right before another reaper shook from the force of a taser.

Satisfied I had created enough chaos to flee, I winged my way up and out of sight. Just before clearing the top of the alley, I glanced back at the collection of reapers. The man in charge stared up at me with narrowed eyes. Wings so white they were blinding unfolded from his back—an angel.

Oh, shit.

He pushed off the ground in pursuit. I hadn't met any angels before, but it was common knowledge they were fast. As fast as a falcon was yet to be determined. I let out a cry of defiance and dove into the night.

As I swooped around buildings and through alleys, his wings beat a steady rhythm against the wind behind me. My pulse raced as quickly as I flew. Despite the pace and tight turns, he gained on me. I swung to the right, hoping to lose him amongst the high rises and parking garages. He might have proved to be swifter than me, but he was also bigger. His size could be a detriment to keeping up with me.

It wasn't, and the angel only seemed to close in on me faster the more I tried to escape. The one time I caught a glimpse of his face, he looked serene, like chasing a falcon through the sky didn't even faze him. In all reality, it probably didn't. But I was tiring quickly and shaken from everything that had occurred that day. I thought fighting off a brood of bloodsuckers was the icing on top, but no, this fucking cake needed a cherry, too.

Salt in the wind called to me like a beacon of hope. I beat my wings harder and headed for the open ocean, where towering clouds gathered earlier, just before sunset. Now, the moon and stars were hidden behind them, darkness blanketing the world below.

I plunged inside the closest cloud, letting the thick mist cool and conceal me, hoping to lose him in the air's near-opacity. I didn't hear his feathery pursuit after a few loops, so I slowed my pace and beat my wings in place, listening as much as I could over my thudding heart.

Not a peep.

I sighed internally. I had lost him, but I needed to be careful where I came out in case he was waiting for me.

Before I made my move, the angel appeared in front of me, close enough to touch. The clouds bent around him as if he repelled them, reforming in his wake. His face betrayed no emotion as he reached out to grab ahold of me.

As his fingers brushed my feathers, I dropped like a stone, folding my wings against my body. The ocean waves rushed toward me. At the last possible moment, I pulled up, the water splashing against my belly. I flew toward land like my life depended on it.

When I was back amongst the buildings, the angel's wings right behind me, I dove for the next garage, gliding inside the lowest level. I shifted and ran on human legs in the same instant, heading for the door that would lead into the next building over. Out of breath and beyond exhausted, I still had enough energy to smirk when I heard him yell in frustration on the other side of the garage. He had assumed I would go through the garage and out where he waited.

A fool for an angel worked in my favor.

If I wanted to be generous, to his credit, he didn't have to know the city inside and out like I did. He knew the skies, and he had his fancy tech toys to get him around town. But I had learned the soft curves and sharp edges of the streets like any good lover would.

That encounter had me so close to ending up in prison. It might still happen, but I wouldn't give up the fight just yet. I still needed answers, and my list of questions kept growing.

A half-hour later and still on foot, I had woven between more buildings and garages than I could count. Under the cover of trees and awnings, I was convinced that I finally lost him. I headed back to the penthouse, shaken and drained.

I WOKE MONDAY morning to bright light streaming through my windows and threw an arm across my face to ward off the sun. The only downside to the penthouse's location was the rising sun, even though I loved it most days. However, most days I wasn't a framed criminal, just a regular one.

"Your boss won't stop calling you," Kit said as she continued to open the electronic curtains. "And now he's calling me as your emergency contact."

I buried my face in my pillow and groaned. I had totally forgotten about my day job. After being sent home for being an absolute train wreck yesterday afternoon, life had become a bit more complicated. If this whole mess left me without my free coffee, I'd be... Well, even more pissed than I already was.

Without raising my face from the pillow, I patted the bedside table, grimacing as pizza crumbs stuck to my palm from a late-night snack after I got home. I found my phone next to the plate. A quick peek at the screen showed five missed calls and nine text messages. It was ten in the morning, and my shift started two hours ago. Damn.

I pressed the button to call my boss back. When he picked up, Isaac immediately went off on a tirade for a full minute.

"I have the flu," I said quickly after he stopped to take a breath.

"Then you have a doctor's note?" Isaac asked, his tone sharp and disbelieving.

"Doctor's note?" Raising my head from the pillow, I glanced at Kit, who rolled her eyes and left the room. For her, faking a note was like falling off a log—any idiot could do it. "Yeah."

"Feel better," he spit out before hanging up.

I winced. I really hated letting my coworkers and regulars down by not showing up but, other than Joe, they didn't know about the supernatural side to life. The Community wasn't out to the rest of the world and had no intentions of coming out again any time soon. What happened after World War II had basically ruined that idea for everyone.

"Get up," Kit's strained voice called from the other room.

"I don't wanna," I complained and buried my head under a pillow. Staying in bed wouldn't help my situation any, but it felt fucking fabulous after the day I had yesterday. I hadn't even told Kit about the vamps and the angel yet.

"V."

Something in her tone made me scramble out of bed, pillows flying everywhere, and jog to the living room. She looked up at me with wide brown eyes filling with water. Tears? Kit never cried.

"It's Tony."

I strode over to the computer she faced, my stomach dropping out beneath me, and looked at the message she pointed to:

Tell the little bird I'm still hungry.

X

Attached was a picture of the piano shop owner, the telepath and my good friend, tied to a piano bench. Blood pooled beneath him from the gushing wounds on his neck.

Xavier had all but ripped the man's throat out. I couldn't tell if Tony was still alive or not when the photo was taken.

My hands—my entire body—shook as I stormed back to my room and ripped off my pajama top and bottoms. I would dress for killing this time. I would dress to slay a motherfucking Master Vampire.

In my closet, I kept two pairs of slim-fit navy cargo pants already stored with weapons and tech goodies galore. After tugging on one pair and adjusting the gear slightly, I pulled on black boots with built-in sheaths, already stocked. I slipped a tight black tank top on that would stay in place with my shoulder holsters.

The Smith & Wesson handguns I placed there were specially designed to shoot fragmenting bullets filled with smaller wooden pellets. Magic ensured the wood wouldn't disintegrate in the firing process, nor upon impact, but would instead spread out inside the victim. The goal being at least one would hit the heart, of course.

Lastly, I clipped a Kit-made wristbow to one of the holster straps, intending to put it on once I got to my destination. The miniature crossbow was a work of art. Designed to fit over my hand like a glove, it fired thin wooden stakes when I clenched the trigger, which I would grip in my palm. Unclenching the trigger would activate the reloading. Kit would make a fortune if she ever decided to sell them to anyone but me.

I slipped on a short-sleeved zip-up hoodie to hide the guns and bow as best I could. No sense causing a panic with the general public, even if I'd be sweating my tits off. Dressed and ready to murder in less than a minute. I was getting good, and now the vampire was going to pay for his crimes.

Kit handed me an earpiece when I went back into the living room. "Keep me in the loop."

I nodded and inserted the tiny two-way microphone into my ear canal.

"And V?"

I glanced back, one hand gripping the sliding glass door to the terrace.

"Time to lift your no killing rule," Kit said, her eyes dry and hardened now.

Resolve strengthened within me. I couldn't agree more.

THE FLIGHT TO Tony's piano shop was quick and virtually thoughtless. I focused solely on the next task at hand—finding and killing Xavier before he could do the same to me. Before that though, I needed to see my friend.

While still in the air above the store, I took a few surveillance loops. No cops, no one from the Community. A closed sign hung on the inside of the window. When I landed, I found the door locked, but it didn't take more than a few seconds to pick. I slipped inside and locked the door again behind me.

The scent of a fight was overwhelming. A metallic tinge of blood blended with the ripeness of vampiric body odor and stung my nostrils. I put an arm to my nose to block it out. It didn't take long to find Tony. He lay on his back along the length of the bench of his favorite grand piano, just like the picture showed.

I knelt by his side, took one of his limp hands in mine, and pressed the back of it to my lips, my mouth dry as a desert. I couldn't believe I had lost yet another person I loved.

"Oh, Tony," my voice broke with the words and my nose tingled, but I refused to cry. Not yet.

His eyelids fluttered. He wasn't gone.

"Kit, he's alive," I gasped out as I pressed the earpiece. "Call an ambulance."

"On it." An eternity that was probably only a few seconds later, she said, "On their way, including one of our own healers."

I let his hand go gently, wanting to leave him as I found him for the paramedics. The Community healer would be able to do what the humans couldn't. Tony might live, or he might die, but either way, Xavier was mine.

"I'll find him, Tony, and I'll kill him." I ground my teeth together. "Or die trying."

CHAPTER 20

Monday Morning

The unmistakable sounds of police and ambulance sirens approached from the next road over as I stepped out of the store. I jogged across the street to the nearest alley, pulling my hood up to hide my blonde hair. Tires squealed to a stop only a moment later, and police surrounded the building with guns drawn.

I ducked into the shadows of the alley until they determined the threat was gone and entered the building. My pulse raced and throbbed in my ears as I watched, but I waited until they wheeled Tony out on a gurney and loaded him into the back of the ambulance before I turned down the two-way alley.

"Kit, where is he?" I didn't have to tell her who I meant. She wanted him dead just as much as I did.

"Working on it."

I took to flight to avoid detection on the streets and give myself some time to think. Whereas walking—or more often stomping—was for letting off steam, some of my best thinking occurred surfing among low-hanging clouds or through the mist of the ocean waves. I chose the waves today, hoping for no surprise encounters with an angel. Flying was both exhilarating and relaxing, and one hell of a difficult concept to explain to those who couldn't do it. Not that I'd had the chance more than once or twice.

Being the last of the phoenixes sounded really cool back in the day, but it had become nothing but a weighted anchor since. What I wouldn't give to be truly free.

My parents had forbidden Mad and me from talking about who and what we were to anyone except them. They had all the answers we needed, they claimed, and everyone else was a threat. Everyone else also thought phoenixes were extinct, which made hiding somewhat easy. My years before they died had been incredibly lonely, and Mad must have felt it even more, being eight years younger than me. He was only ten when they left us.

Oh, Mad. What happened to you? My heart wanted to flee from my chest to escape the inevitable pain. *Not yet, little brother, but soon.* Once I cleared my name, then I could focus on the truth of his death.

I flew south, aiming for the Cape Florida Lighthouse— a favorite flight destination of mine. I didn't want to go too far from the mainland, so I could stay within hearing range. When Kit tracked him down, I wanted to be ready to swoop back and rip Xavier to shreds. There would be no stopping today, but it would be a comforting sight.

Maybe I had turned to an acquisitions lifestyle because of my parents' ironclad control. They weren't bad parents; in fact, they were downright awesome. But anyone would start to break and rebel after years of following such rigid rules and routines. I was rarely allowed to shift without permission, and that usually only occurred during a training session.

Tracking an object down gave me a reason to take flight on a whim and skim the waves with the edges of my wings as I did now, with no one around to tell me no. The thrill of getting away with a job sure didn't hurt either. The rush of adrenaline beating through my limbs was undeniably freeing, and no one controlled me—not even Xavier.

I would destroy him.

I screeched my rage into the sky. The crisp ocean breeze rustled its way through my feathers once again before I wheeled up, around the lighthouse, and back into the city.

Time to hunt.

I would be able to hear Kit when she had a location— even the earpieces stayed in place when I shifted—but I wouldn't be able to respond since returning a communication required me to touch the device. Not to mention Kit didn't understand my falcon cries. For now, I'd use my avian vision to do my own tracking.

Using my ability to detect ultraviolet light and objects at crazy distances wasn't usually necessary for my kind of hunting when I just needed a quick bite of a fish to refuel.

Still, it was exceptionally advantageous when hunting vamps. Unlike reapers, who were also technically dead, vampires emitted a small number of ultraviolet rays, especially after a feed. But it was very clearly different from humans and other Community members, like the light was tainted with blood.

"Got a bead on him near Jackson Memorial," Kit's voice crackled through to my ear. "He hides his movements well, but I was able to find a condo building he owns off of Miami River. I'll send you the address, but you'll probably be able to spot it from the air."

I let out a victory cry and winged west toward the river. I would have found his nest eventually, after hours of scouring the city block by block, leaving me exhausted and useless. Having a tech genius as a best friend and partner made things go a whole lot faster.

Building a nest near a hospital was gross but also super useful to the vampire clans, and most of them had some sort of working arrangement with hospital management. Keeping the clans fed and happy also meant the death toll would be way down in the area, a requirement of the DEA.

The building was easy to identify as a nest once I found it. It was swarming with vampires' ultraviolet light. If I thought *I* had a lot of money, Xavier out-zeroed my bank account ten times over. Owning an entire eight-story luxury condominium on the banks of Miami River screamed wealth. That must be what living for a millennium or two did for you. Thick foliage and tall palm trees surrounded the building, hiding the creatures from prying eyes. On the ground, anyway.

I alighted on the roof and shifted forms.

"Damn, girl," I said quietly. "Maybe we need to upgrade my digs."

It was a joke, of course. Nothing beat the view of the water from my penthouse. After pulling out one of my handguns, I crouched down and crept to the roof's edge. I held the gun ready, just in case anything popped up.

"Please tell me you're not just going to charge in there," Kit's exasperated tone was evident even through the earpiece.

"No, I'm not that stupid," I said, though I had been questioning my intelligence quite a bit lately. "I'll wait him out."

I wasn't too concerned with vampires hanging around outside in the middle of the day, so I glanced down over the edge. Before I pulled my head back, I counted three bloodsuckers along the perimeter who stayed in the shade and amongst the foliage. There were probably a few more I didn't see.

"I've been doing some research on his normal nocturnal haunts," Kit said. "He never goes anywhere without at least one full brood who could pass for human surrounding him."

I cursed beneath my breath. Facing six of the younger ones had left me on my knees about to become their dinner. Imagine what twelve of the older kind could do. I chewed on my bottom lip.

How the hell was I going to get him away from his brood? Or even part of it. I had been ambushed in the alley before, but maybe if I were the one doing the ambushing this time and with proper weapons, I'd be able to take more down.

But facing a Master Vampire wasn't the same as dealing with the older vamp from earlier. A Master had at least a millennium or more to hone his skills and shed his humanity.

I clenched my empty fist as I felt my options slipping through my fingers, as if I could somehow hold on to them. I didn't want to wait long enough to learn his habits and find the cracks in his armor. I wanted to swoop in and kill the motherfucker.

"You have another option," Kit said, her voice contemplative.

"I'm all ears."

"Thane."

"He's locked up," I said.

"Never stopped you before."

I sat back on one heel, the other sole flat on the ground as I considered what she was proposing. "Holy shit. If I could pull that off, my charge for contracts could go through the roof."

Cha-motherfucking-ching. If I survived this whole ordeal, my next few checks would go straight to Tony.

"Not like you need the money."

"Can you pull up schematics?" I asked.

"Way ahead of you."

My phone buzzed against my leg where I had it tucked into a pocket. I pulled it out and studied the images she sent. "You're kidding me. They have windows in their cells? What is it, a luxury prison?"

"The agency has never had to worry about escape before," she said. "And the windows are tiny by human or angel standards."

"So I can get in and out, but what about Thane?" I squinted at the maps, following the green arrows she added to indicate the exit route. "That's the only way?"

"Yep."

It seemed simple enough in theory: fly in, convince Thane to join me, then follow the stairs out. In actuality, the only simple part was flying in. I had no idea how Thane would feel about escaping and whether or not he would be on board with joining me as I went after Xavier. I had a sneaking suspicion he would if I dangled the jewelry box in front of him like a carrot. The reaper wanted it bad.

There was just that one little bit about convincing him to fight his way out. There was zero percent chance we'd be able to waltz out of there, even with Kit creating chaos on another floor. Neither of us would need to kill anyone, I hoped, but I wasn't sure how Thane would feel about potentially hurting his peers. I didn't really know much about him as a person except for what his touch did to me and my lady bits.

I took a deep breath and tucked my phone away. "Alright. Time to plan a breakout."

CHAPTER 21

Sunday Midday

I knew where Miami's DEA office was located in the government quarter downtown—all the members of the Community knew to avoid it, either from superstition or experience. Not that being there meant you would be randomly arrested or anything—not unless you had something to hide, which, let's face it, we all did—but being around that many grim reapers gave most people the heebie-jeebies, like death was contagious.

As far I knew, in most cases it wasn't.

I slipped my gun back into its holster then shifted into a bird on Xavier's condo roof, taking to the skies. If I was going to bring down the city's Master Vampire without getting myself killed in the process, I would need help from the only other ally I had at the moment. Well, I hoped Thane was still my ally. If I had misinterpreted or imagined the tilt of his head in the alley, he might not be. He might think I just up and left him to take the fall for both of us.

The agency building would have precautions in place to track any unregistered members of the Community or uses of magic. Kit would be the real hero of the day, if you could even call us that to begin with considering we were breaking into a magical fortress to basically kidnap a reaper and force him to help me kill someone. A someone who was also a monster, but still a someone.

Regardless of our intentions, Kit would attack their security system with hers, buying me enough of a distraction and time to get to Thane and get us both back out. To start, she would lift the security off his cell window, letting her test their defenses while also allowing me access inside.

The midday sun beat down on my feathers as I landed on the sill to his seventh-floor cell and peered inside. As predicted, Thane was alone in the tiny room, which was built with thick walls between him and the next cell over and hopefully soundproof. The only piece of furniture was the narrow cot he sat on.

Craning my neck to see through the bars of the door, I spied two reaper guards playing on their phones behind a desk. Another reaper strolled in to drop off some paperwork before disappearing out the door again. Satisfied, I let out a low ee-chup, also known as an inquisitive bird sound.

Thane looked up from the book he read on his cot and smiled. "Aren't you a pretty thing?"

I hopped down to a corner of the room where I would be hidden from the guards and shifted into my human form. Staying in a low crouch, I whispered, "Thanks for the compliment."

Thane's eyebrows had lifted, but other than that, he kept his surprise to himself. "I didn't get a good look at you before you swooped off last night. Welcome to my humble abode."

"Not for long." I peered around his leg to make sure the guards stayed put. So far, so good. "I need your help."

"I'm a bit preoccupied right now," he said, amusement dancing across his features. "You really pissed Adam off. I've never seen him so angry."

Ah, so that angel was his boss.

"Yeah, well, falcons are fast. He can't get too mad at the biology he thinks his god created. Anyway, I can get you out of here."

"And get me into even deeper shit? I'll pass." He returned to his book, *Zen and the Art of Motorcycle Maintenance*. Interesting choice for a reaper.

"We can clear both our names by taking down Xavier." I urged my voice to remain calm and quiet despite my rising temper.

"It's a life sentence for me and a suicide mission for you."

"Not if we do it together," I said through clenched teeth. I had known it would be tough to convince him, but knowing it ahead of time didn't mean I would be able to handle it calmly now. "But if you don't come with me, I'm going to blame this all on you."

Thane looked up at me with a gleam in his eyes. I couldn't tell if it was a good or bad gleam. "Blackmail, huh?"

I shrugged. "Whatever works."

"How exactly do you see your blackmail working when I'm stuck in here? They'll know I didn't do whatever it is you're about to do." He closed the book and smiled at me.

I smiled right back at the smug bastard. "Kit is a technological genius and a hacker. It won't be difficult, especially since I plan to open this door and fight my way out anyway. Whether you stay in this cell or not is up to you."

He stared at me. "You're kind of crazy, aren't you?"

"I need one more thing," I said. Let him draw whatever conclusion he wanted about my mental state, as long as I got his agreement.

"Because blackmail, fleeing custody, and killing a member of the Community isn't enough?" Thane's sarcasm was so thick, I could just about taste it. Bitter, like an ice-cold IPA. I would definitely be cracking one of those bad boys open when this disaster finally ended.

"After we've cleared our names, I need you to find out what you can about my brother's death."

He considered me for a moment, his expression softening. "If we survive, I'll see what I can do."

I put out my hand and he shook it, the corners of his lips curving up. We both knew a reaper's word was enough, and the butterflies in my stomach twirled and spun in response to his tiny smirk. I held on to the heat of his touch a tad longer than I needed to, but hey, I might die with what we were about to attempt. A little comfort before death sounded good to me.

So what if I could resurrect myself?

"Deal," he said, mimicking my words from the last time we made a deal. Only he made it seem cute. Goddamn it.

"Kit, let's fly," I said, touching my earpiece.

"On your marks," she said.

As her fingers typed out a whirlwind of commands, I drew one of my knives and offered it to Thane. He shook his head. I guess he didn't want to hurt his friends, if they called themselves that. I kept the knife for myself and withdrew a set of brass knuckles, which I slipped on my right hand.

"Get set," Kit said.

The knuckles and knife were coated with a fast-acting sedative for scenarios just like these. Reapers had been human once and would still react to the drug, albeit for a much shorter time. But like I said, I wasn't a killer. Putting obstacles to sleep with a hard knock to the head or a small slice to the arm worked just as well for me.

"Go!"

Alarms blared throughout the cell block and echoed through the rest of the building. A breath later and Thane's cell door slid to the side.

"She's good," he said as I passed him.

"The best."

One of the guards already had a phone in hand at the desk, while the other was on his feet and had his gun raised as he checked each cell. Lucky for me, he had his back turned. With the handle of my knife, I cracked him over the head before giving him a minor slice across his arm with a sharp edge of the knuckles. Never hurt to be sure. As he fell to the ground, I whirled to face the other guard.

Thane stood face-to-face with him, one hand over the man's mouth, the other holding the back of his neck in an odd-looking hold. Thane's eyes had gone completely black, and he chanted. The other reaper's eyes rolled into the back of his head, and Thane set him down gently in the chair.

"I'm not sure whether I should be impressed or jealous," I said, raising my eyebrows.

He gave his now-familiar smirk before we headed down the cell block hallway toward the emergency stairwell, ignoring the shouts from the other inmates, all members of the Community. They actually deserved to be in there. Probably. Either way, no time to stop and find out. Worrying about myself and Thane was all I could handle right now.

As the door to the stairs shut behind us, I caught the distant yells from reapers as they exited the elevator. They'd be checking each floor to determine where the threat came from.

We ran down the steps two or three at a time. Seven flights would get us all the way to the lobby, then another one down to exit through the garage. No one crossed our paths until we had three flights left. The door opened and two reapers ran in, surprise written across their faces when they caught sight of us.

"Thane?" asked one of the men, lowering his weapon slightly.

I didn't hesitate, mostly because I was running down the steps too fast to stop. Using the end of the rail as leverage, I swung out with the last step, and my boot connected with his jaw. His head flew to the side to slam into the wall, and he slumped to the ground.

The other reaper turned his aim on me, but I had landed in a crouch by then. I threw myself forward as he fired. I completed my tumble and came back to my feet. I gave his face a solid right jab with my brass knuckles. The hit stunned him momentarily but didn't knock him down or break the skin.

He raised his hands to aim at me again. I don't care what anyone says—staring down the barrel of a gun, especially one in such close range and not likely to miss, is a terrifying sight, sometimes paralyzing. Despite my years of training, even I wasn't immune to the paralysis, and I froze, my eyes opening wide.

But he forgot about Thane.

In all honesty, I did, too. Thane stood behind him chanting, one hand moving to cover the reaper's mouth, the other across the back of his neck. The reaper's eyes rolled up into his head, and Thane laid him carefully on the step leading up.

"Let's go," he said and headed down again.

I tucked my knife away and slid down the rail after him. "No wonder everyone is afraid of you guys."

"Not you, though?"

"I don't have much to lose anymore." I shrugged.

His glance felt like a weight on me as I took another rail down. I was sure he'd ask me about my comment later—didn't mean I had to answer it, though. One more flight, and we would be out. I pushed through the door leading into the garage and came to a stumbling halt.

A line of reapers faced us, blocking our exit with guns aimed to kill.

CHAPTER 22

Sunday Midday

G ame's over," called a female voice we both knew. I should have known. Fucking Sophia. She strode forward past the other reapers—I counted ten including her—her black kitten heels clacking against the garage's concrete floor.

Personally, I would have gone for a few more inches of height. Her petite stature wasn't super intimidating.

"You've sure made a bigger mess of things," she said, her sharp green eyes fixed on Thane, who had stopped next to me. She crossed her arms over her sleeveless black dress. "I was just about to get your charges dropped."

He frowned. "You didn't sound like you were on my side back in the alley."

"I've done some research since then," Sophia said, her gaze flicking to me. "Ms. Neill has been quite the bad girl. May have killed her own brother. Don't get caught up in her mess, Thane. Time to choose the right side." She tilted her head, indicating he move to stand next to her.

Thane put an arm out to stop me as I stepped forward, rage fueling my steps. I clenched my fists at my side, the unpoisoned underside of the brass knuckles digging into my right palm. Did she really think I killed my own brother? My only family? The boy I loved more than anyone else in the world? My body trembled as I fought to keep control of myself and not explode on the spot. The fact that anyone, especially a woman like Sophia, could think I had anything to do with his death made me see red.

She was a dead woman. A *real* dead woman.

Every inch of my skin burned with rage, my chest tightening. I looked up at Thane, all the more furious that my eyes were watering. Not from sadness, but with anger. I had lived three years, three long fucking years, thinking I wasn't good enough for Maddox. Feeling like I had failed him, that I didn't the signs, when in reality, someone stole his life from me.

Thane knew that, and he knew how much it had stunned me when he revealed the truth. And now this woman—who I once helped by getting my hands on some information she needed for a case via not-so-legal practices—stood before me questioning *my* morality. This was how she repaid me?

The reapers knew about my alter ego now, and it was entirely possible that Sophia was the one to reveal my identity and not the angels like I thought. Nothing was holding me back from broadcasting her deep dark secret—except for one thing.

I was a better person than her. Not by much, maybe, but I still wouldn't stoop to her level.

Thane's eyes questioned me, and I answered with my own, fury and pain beyond measure vying for space in my heart. A tear slid down my cheek. He used a thumb to wipe it away, a brand searing across my skin beneath his touch.

"Are you with me?" I whispered so quietly, I barely heard myself.

"Thane, don't be stupid," Sophia said, shifting with impatience. I was sure she hadn't heard me, but she knew we were connecting even without words. I was sure it made her nervous, seeing how she thought she had some claim on this sexier-than-sin man. She put her hands on her hips. "There's no choice here."

The reaper in front of me gave an almost imperceptible nod in my direction.

Before turning to face Sophia, I whispered, "Then cover your ears."

I didn't wait to see if he obeyed, and I didn't know that would actually help if he did. Clenching my fists in front of me, I took a deep breath, opened my mouth, and let loose an eardrum-shattering scream. The falcon screech was one of the phoenix abilities I did my best to keep hidden, and I had only used it once before outside of training.

Gale-force winds surged out from my mouth, whooshing into and past the reapers, forcing them to raise their arms or close their eyes against the stirred-up debris. The blast of sonar-like energy made the concrete ground rumble, and the reapers stumbled backward. One lost his balance entirely and fell to the ground. Car alarms blared through the enclosed space, set off either by the pitch of my screech or the rumbling earth.

Before the reapers recovered from the unexpected form of resistance, I raised my hands, palms up, and called forth the fire writhing in my core. It was always there, ever since my first birth, begging to be unleashed. Releasing it felt as natural as breathing or blinking. The magical flame slithered down my body and snaked across the ground, forming a red-hot line between the reapers and me. It melted the concrete with the intensity of its heat. I rarely needed to use this much magic, and never to the extent I did now.

I set the lance on fire, building the line separating us into a blaze until it became an inferno that licked the ceiling, blackening the concrete wherever it touched. When I released the magic completely, a wall of living fire blocked Thane and me from the reapers' view. Shouts and cries of pain came from the other side, muffled by the roaring of the flames. I grabbed Thane's hand and ran toward the ramp leading out.

"What the hell was that?" he asked as we sprinted up the incline.

"Escape first, questions later." I pulled his arm toward a side street once we exited the garage.

A black sedan with equally dark windows and no license plates squealed to a halt next to the curb. Kit's welcome face peered out as the window rolled down. "Get in."

I didn't hesitate, and thankfully neither did Thane. Kit didn't even wait for the door to close before she revved the engine and tore off down the street, leaving one reaper who had made it out of the garage coughing in the exhaust behind us. Soot from my fire covered his face and hair.

"Okay, now you need to answer my question," Thane said. "That's not magic like I've ever seen before."

"There's probably a lot of magic out there you haven't seen yet," I said through gulping breaths, trying to calm my racing heart.

"How much did you use?" Kit asked as she swerved around the line of traffic.

"I think all of it." My limbs were starting to feel a bit fuzzy and tingly.

"Fuck, V," she said, her deep brown eyes glancing at me in the rearview mirror. "You gonna make it?"

"Make it?" Thane asked, his eyebrows pulling together. "What does that mean?"

"Probably not." I gave him a rueful smile, just now noticing a trail of blood leading out of his ear. My screech must have popped his ear drum. "Magic has limits, and I…" My vision spun, and the world toppled sideways as the backseat rushed up to greet me.

"Veronica!"

I WOKE IN THE pitch black of night, though the moon's pale light reflecting off buildings across from mine showed I was in my penthouse bedroom. Passing out after depleting immense amounts of magic was such a huge downside to using it. My head throbbed.

"Hello?" I croaked out.

A figure rose from a chair in the corner and approached. Thane. He held a cup to my lips and helped me sit up enough to sip the water. I pushed the cup away after a few more sips, my eyelids fluttering shut as exhaustion tugged me back down.

"Aren't you the most tempting mystery?" he murmured, a cold washcloth brushing across my forehead before I slipped into a deep sleep.

WHEN I WOKE again, I was alone in my room. A quick glance under the sheets revealed that I was in a fresh set of pajamas, a silk camisole and shorts set in a blush rose color. One of my favorites. Kit better have been the one to put that on.

Actually, I didn't really care. If it was Thane, I hoped he enjoyed the view—the pervert.

My inner flame swirled happily, replenished once again after the rest. As I was about to tell Thane before my body gave out, magic users didn't have an infinite supply of the stuff. We needed time to regenerate, to replenish our wells.

Reapers were an exception, of course. The only one that I knew of, which is why businesses like Luciana's *The Witch's Brew* did so well. Community members like witches and mages could store some of their magic outside themselves for use later. The healing potion I used after the manticore encounter was one such example.

I had drained my supply to escape the reapers, which resulted in my subsequent blackout and middle-of-the-night migraine. Using magic wasn't free, and it didn't wait for a suitable time before taking its toll. With any luck, Kit had filled Thane in on these nuances from her own point of view so I could avoid explaining my particular kind of magic.

After stumbling out of bed and allowing myself a moment to let the world spin, I found the two of them in the living room, talking quietly.

"Don't your kind come with trackers?" I asked, padding to the coffee maker at the end of the kitchen counter. The half-full carafe was still hot. Hallelujah. "How long was I out?

"About a day," Kit said. "But don't worry about trackers. You know both my magic and technical wards have made this place invisible, even to manticores this time."

"She also cut that out of the back of my neck just to be safe." Thane nodded at a piece of shattered glass with a red tint on my coffee table. The tracking device—and blood. Lovely.

"Ouch." I poured myself a cup of coffee and carried it over to the living room.

He shrugged. "Reapers heal pretty fast."

I knew that, of course, but I kept it to myself. Knowing their healing abilities was exactly why I went for knockouts with the reapers on the stairs. Shaking the brain was the most effective way to take one down without killing him. That was pretty true for most species, I would wager.

"You didn't tell me about your upper-class digs," he said, lounging on one end of my L-shaped couch, his arms spread out along the back.

"You didn't tell me your boss was an angel." Having an angel for a direct boss meant a reaper was close to earning his wings. He might have just forfeited them by escaping custody, and I might have felt slightly guilty for blackmailing him, but only slightly. After all, he still had a choice, and I planned to clear his name when all was said and done.

He smirked. "Fair."

"What'd I miss?" I tucked one leg beneath the other as I sat on a chair and held my cup in both hands. A rich, earthy scent drifted up from the mug. Heaven.

Thane and Kit shared a glance.

"What's that all about?" I raised an eyebrow and sipped my hot beverage.

"You received a letter." Kit stood and walked to the penthouse entryway. She picked up an envelope from the console table and brought it over to me.

"It came here?" I asked through a cough as I nearly choked on my coffee. "I thought we were invisible."

"No, it was left under the door of your other place," Kit said. "I went over when the wards activated with a disturbance."

"Not alone, I hope."

"The wards indicated there was no threat," she said. "Thane stayed here to make sure you were safe."

I hid my burning cheeks behind my oversized mug. I wasn't embarrassed by any means, but I had super conflicting feelings about having this highly attractive, powerful man watch over me while I slept.

I kind of liked it. Maybe he *had* been the one to change my clothes.

Kit stared at me.

"What?" I asked, shifting as if she could read my thoughts. She couldn't, for the record, but I still felt caught in the act.

"Open the damn thing."

"Oh, right." I set down my mug and slid a finger under the envelope flap then pulled out the folded paper inside. The note had been written in red ink on a piece of parchment similar to papyrus. I leaned closer and sniffed, my nostrils immediately flaring out with distaste.

Nope, not ink. Blood.

Dearest Falcon,

Please accept this humble invitation to meet with me on neutral grounds. I'll be at el Cuento de Sirenas *by 6pm sharp. Don't be late. Oh, and bring the Reaper.*

Sincerely,

X

"It's him," I told them, thankful he hadn't used flayed skin in place of old paper. "He wants to meet."

"It's a trap," Thane said.

"Of course it is."

"What are you going to do?" Kit asked.

"The only thing I can do," I said, setting the paper down on the table and getting back to my feet. My legs wobbled beneath me.

"Meet with a Master Vampire."

CHAPTER 23

Monday Afternoon

"Why would you agree to meet with him?" Thane asked as I rose from my chair and walked back to the kitchen.

I set my mug down on the counter next to the coffee maker. Pursing my lips, I considered washing the cup but decided against it. If I survived the meeting with my freedom intact, then doing the dishes would be the start of my lifelong penance. And if I didn't survive, then who the fuck cared?

"Because he'll think he has the upper hand." I turned and leaned back against the counter, crossing my arms.

"Men like him, especially old as fuck men like him, think of women as the weaker sex. He won't see me coming."

Thane smirked, but it was that adorable smirk that made the butterflies flutter around inside. "I get the feeling not many men do."

I glanced at the clock, partly to hide my return smirk. It was 4:47 in the afternoon. Just over an hour to prepare and get to *el Cuento de Sirenas*, which was only about twenty minutes away by car according to GPS.

I looked Thane over from head to toe, appraising his clothes for fighting purposes, and nodded. "We both need to change."

My current outfit was nowhere near functional for hunting, nor being let into a restaurant. Well, they would probably allow me inside in my silk pajamas. This was Miami after all, but somewhere along the way, Thane's shirt had collected dirt and soot. The soot from the fire back at the garage, but the dirt was his own damn fault.

After a quick change, I came back out of my room, now wearing a cream-colored silk top with thin straps. The fabric fell loosely until it cinched at my natural waist, showing off the curves of my hips while also concealing the tiny derringer loaded with sharpened wooden bullets. I didn't know enough about vampires' magical biology to understand why a stake through the heart did the trick, but I was always prepared. When I knew I would be facing them, anyway.

I also wore a pair of tight-fitting, dark blue jeans and booties that allowed me to tuck a small wooden boot knife into each. I tossed Thane a simple black button-down dress shirt.

"Dare I ask why you keep men's clothes in your home?" He grinned at me before pulling his soot-stained shirt over his head.

I bit my lip as I enjoyed the sight of his defined chest and stomach a little bit too much. The party boy had obviously taken care of himself during his living years. His washboard abs and deep tan had survived his death and resulted in a very tempting V pointing toward his—

"I want you in contact the whole time," Kit's voice broke through my train of thought, which was on a crash course to nowhere smart.

"Definitely." Giving myself a little internal shake, I realized I hadn't answered Thane's question. Luckily for me, he stood to drape his soiled shirt on a metal chair and didn't notice me staring. "I kept some of my parents' things after they passed."

To avoid going down that conversational path, I focused my gaze on my partner, who had moved back to her computer set up on the dining room table. "Were you able to find anything out about this restaurant that might help us?"

After slipping the new shirt on, Thane buttoned the front, hiding any tempting views from my periphery. Most of them, anyway. The fit was a bit tight across his chest and biceps; my father had had a slimmer build than the reaper.

"The place isn't open yet," Kit said, brushing her braids behind a shoulder as she leaned against the back of the chair. "He's attempting to purchase the building from the current owners. But it's in the middle of a busy row of restaurants, which means he wants to talk business with you. That or he's getting cocky."

I rolled my eyes. "Whatever happened to just fighting your way to the top? A good duel never hurt anyone."

Kit stared at me. "A good duel kills one or both of the people involved."

Shrugging off her comment because I couldn't focus on negative facts just yet—no matter how accurate—I moved to the kitchen cabinets next to the refrigerator and opened them. If someone were paying close enough attention, she would notice the shelves weren't quite as deep as they should have been. I ran my hand underneath one set at waist height and pressed the hidden button, so smooth I barely felt it.

With a soft click and a hiss, the shelves moved out and to the sides, revealing the true storage within. A beautiful assortment of weapons stood before me, and I sensed Thane moving in to get a better view.

"Time to suit up."

I eyed Thane's outfit again before deciding on a slightly larger gun than my derringer—a Smith & Wesson that also held fragmenting bullets filled with wooden pellets. The weapon would be hidden in his waistband under his shirt using the holster I passed to him next. I also offered him a slim sheath equipped with a wooden stake for each bicep, which he could tuck away beneath his sleeves. A tight fit, but the dark color of the fabric helped. With any luck, his reaper hold move would be enough, but I didn't want to leave this encounter to chance.

I started to close the shelves but stopped when a glint of metal caught my eye.

Reaching back inside, I withdrew the necklace: a talisman with my family crest stamped on the front. To anyone else, it would just look like a falcon. I rubbed my thumb along the design, allowing my heart to ache for just a moment for all that I had lost. I wasn't sure the magic would work on his kind, but I wouldn't lose anyone else if I could help it.

Turning toward Thane, I beckoned him closer. "Wear this, and don't ask questions."

Surprisingly, he didn't protest. I unhooked the clasp and wrapped the chain around his neck, having to rise up on my tiptoes a bit to secure it behind him. His hands drifted to my hips as if to steady me, but the way his eyes met mine as I drew back spoke to other intentions. His fingers seared against my bare skin as he tightened his grip.

We stood there, face-to-face, and I couldn't help but think of the much too quick kiss we'd shared, even if it had been so he could handcuff me. My gaze drifted to his mouth. His lips had felt so warm against mine, so alive, sending electric currents through every fiber of my being. I wanted to feel it again.

A cough behind Thane broke us apart.

"Another time, kids," Kit said and handed me an earpiece.

"You're not coming?" he asked.

"No." She turned and walked back to her desk.

Thane raised an eyebrow at me in question, but it was Kit who answered. "I don't use magic anymore, and my physical skills only get me so far with other members of the Community, especially vampires."

"A witch who doesn't use magic?" he asked with a smirk. He didn't know her past or else he wouldn't be making light of it.

Kit returned to her computer and started typing, and I pulled Thane toward the door.

"What was that all about?" he asked when we reached the elevator.

"Kit was one of the witches who helped the fae return to the shadows after the outing in Italy," I said. The doors opened, and we stepped inside the elevator car. "It's a long story, and hers to tell, but let's just say the cleanup wasn't pretty."

That was a huge understatement, of course; the witches had covered up a massacre. But this wasn't the time nor place to get into history and politics. If she wanted to, Kit could tell him the story another day.

The elevator doors shut, and we rode the rest of the way down in silence.

CHAPTER 24

Monday Evening

El Cuento de Sirenas, The Mermaid's Tale restaurant with a cute play-on-words name, was located right on Biscayne Bay. It would be a prime spot once it opened. The almost-able-to-pass-for-human (if I squinted) vampire at the door led us to the back of the otherwise-empty restaurant and out onto the terrace, lit with Edison bulb string lights above our heads. A crisp breeze brushed my ponytail off my skin, where the ends of my hair started to stick. The humidity never seemed to cease in Miami, not even at night.

The restaurants on either side also had outdoor seating, and the bustling sights and sounds of dinners being served and tables cleaned provided a soothing backdrop. It would have been reassuring as a rendezvous point had I not been meeting a Master Vampire hellbent on acquiring *me*.

I had never met Xavier in person before because if I had, I would have immediately recognized what he was and never done business with him. He sat on a chair with one leg draped lazily over the other. I could have kicked myself for how stupid I'd been. Instead, I would have to let Xavier do it for me right before I put a stake through his heart. One kick and then poof.

Vampires often became ridiculously good looking in the centuries after their deaths. Regaining their human features took some time—make that a lot of time and a lot of food. The blood they drank shaped and molded them, recreating them from the inside out. Part of their evolving nature was to become attractive to their prey. Similar to the orchid mantis, they looked good enough to eat, only they were the ones who ended up doing the feasting.

Xavier was no exception to this biological evolution.

In fact, he was near the top of the food chain as a Master, and I hadn't met one as old as he appeared to be. And by appeared to be old, I meant beyond beautiful.

Hair the vibrant hues of autumn fell in soft curls around his ears to tickle his smooth chin. Vampires stopped growing hair in death, but they never seemed to lose the amount on their heads. I imagine whether or not to cut their hair or trim their beards became quite a dilemma.

The Master Vampire's face was all sharp angles and lines, a striking latte-colored painting meant to distract from the hardness in his dark brown eyes and the pointed canines hiding just behind very kissable lips. To complete his undeniable sex appeal, he wore sand-colored linen slacks and a matching blazer over a blue floral-patterned shirt with the sleeves rolled up together. And because we were in Miami, his loafers were the same azure hue as his shirt.

Fashionably loud and proud of it.

I would have almost said it wouldn't be so bad being enslaved to a man that good looking, except I saw through the facade to the monster beneath.

Xavier stood as we approached, his expression unreadable. "You're late."

The vampire who led us in glanced between his Master and us before scampering away. A wise idea, and I kind of wished I could follow him.

"It's 6:01," I said, waiting for his invitation to sit. I knew basic etiquette, and with a vampire as old as this one, etiquette was akin to godliness. Mine only went so far, though. "You're lucky I didn't have to do much with my hair."

He stared at me for another moment, his eyes calculating, before he grinned. His canines flashed in the fading daylight.

"Lucky, yes. Please, sit." His voice held the slightest accent, but it wasn't Spanish like I had expected. I couldn't place it yet. He motioned to the two chairs across from him at the table, the only one set up in the entire restaurant.

Thane and I took our seats, and for a few blissful moments, the only sounds were the gentle lapping of the waves on the side of the building and the pop music from the restaurant closest to us.

"So, my beautiful Falcon," Xavier's eyes sparkled, "or should I call you Veronica?"

"V is fine," I said, meeting his gaze straight on.

"V," he repeated, emphasizing the sound with a soft bite of his bottom lip. "It seems our arrangement has come to an end."

His lips drew my gaze as he talked. They were so full and red, not so much like he wore lipstick, but full of *life*—an odd thing to think of someone who had died so long ago. I stared at his lips and the way he wet them ever-so-slightly with the tip of his tongue, the way they remained parted in between words. I wanted to feel those lips on all parts of me, his tongue exploring the hidden parts of me, before he thrust his coc—

I shook myself and met his knowing gaze. Goddamn vampires. "If you would be so kind, stay the fuck out of my head. No mind games."

"But what a pretty little head you have." Xavier's eyes held a dangerous glint. "A golden cage with your name on it awaits in my bedroom."

I narrowed my eyes. "You agreed to give me a week."

"I did, didn't I?" He tapped the arms of his chair as he considered me. "However, it's no longer possible for you to acquire the jewelry box."

"You doubt my skills?" We already knew he had the box, but he didn't know that yet. I kept my hands folded together in my lap to keep from fidgeting. It was hard.

"I do."

I raised an eyebrow. "Why?"

"Because I have the box." Xavier's smile turned malicious.

Thane leaned forward. "If you have it, then why haven't you used it?"

I frowned, annoyed that I still didn't know what the box actually did.

"I didn't get it for me," the vampire said, waving a hand dismissively. "I have no desire to grow wings."

"What the hell does this box do?" I asked, unable to restrain myself. What kind of wings were we talking about here?

Amusement flickered across Xavier's face. "Lover boy here didn't tell you?"

"If he did, would I be asking?" I ground my teeth together. I hated being caught unaware about anything, especially by a vampire.

"It's forbidden to discuss," Thane said, shrugging. "Let's move on to you returning it and the stolen soul."

"Only forbidden for your kind," Xavier said with a wink. "The *tanets angelov* is as old as time. It's the original Pandora's Box, as it also releases unexpected evil into the world. Depending on who you ask, of course."

"That doesn't make sense with your comment about growing wings," I said. Most humans and Community members alike would jump at the chance to grow a pair of wings. Why would that be seen as evil?

"Oh, but it does," the vampire said eagerly. "The box grants the user a specific set of wings—angel wings. A one-way ticket to heaven and a seat at his holiness's feet."

Pieces clicked into place, but it was far from a complete puzzle. For a Master Vampire, more angels would equate to even more of a pestilence on the earth, or unexpected evil as he put it. But he didn't want the wings, which meant he got them for another reason. Or another someone.

Was he working with Aamon? Very few demons could grow wings, after all, and I was sure the majority of them would jump at the chance to leave hell. I just didn't know why a vampire would be willing to steal such an item for a demon. What would Xavier be getting out of the deal? And why take the soul?

Maybe it wasn't for Aamon. I still wasn't fully caught up on fae politics, but angel wings would all but ensure dominance for whichever side snatched them up. Broderick hadn't been in the wrong place at the wrong time, then; he wanted the wings. If the duke got his hands on the box, then he could crush the fae queen and her followers like bugs.

Vampires didn't get along with most of the Community, but their deep animosity toward the fae wasn't a secret from anyone. Xavier would be doing his entire species a favor by ridding the human world of the fae, and siding with the fae queen would make that a reality.

No matter who Xavier had stolen the box for, it made complete sense that Thane would want it as well. The *tanets angelov* ensured a fast track to earning his own set of wings, even though I hadn't taken him for a cheater. I dug my one of my nails into my palm to keep my expression calm. Like I said before, I didn't exactly do the whole people thing well. I almost laughed at myself for falling for Thane's act, except I was beyond pissed at him for playing me for a fool.

"Who did you give the box to?" Thane asked, his voice strained.

"That's the kicker, isn't it? You'd never guess. But don't worry, you won't have to." Xavier turned his gaze on me, his eyes darkening. "Before we get to that, however, we need to discuss our arrangement."

I swallowed hard. "I want my full week."

His smile was anything but kind. "I'm feeling generous. You may have your last few days. But if you try to escape your failure, you'll regret it for years to come." A flicker of red flashed behind his pupils—blood rising in excitement. "Do you understand?"

"Yes," I managed to get out as my lungs constricted, making it almost difficult to breathe. I didn't doubt he would make me regret even asking for the week.

"Let's go meet the soon-to-be proud new owner of angel wings, shall we?" Xavier slapped his hands down on the arms of his chair and stood, motioning us to follow.

Thane and I exchanged a glance, but we really didn't have a choice. He wanted the box and wings, and I needed to kill the vampire. If I didn't, I would need to find a way out of there and run and continue running for the rest of my long life. I kept my eyes open for possible escape routes as we followed Xavier through the restaurant's main room and passed the steel jungle of an empty kitchen, complete with brand-new stoves and countertops.

My mind raced as fast as my pulse. I still hadn't come up with any reason why a vampire would work with a demon, and the more I thought about it, the more I knew it had to be the fae queen. Fae blood was poisonous to vampires. The longer the fae mingled with humans and created half-bloods, the less food was available for the undead.

I had once considered purchasing a vial of fae blood on the black-market, a highly illegal transaction, to coat my wooden stakes and bullets. But back then, I hadn't been quite ready to sign my death warrant if I got caught. If only I knew then what I knew now.

Xavier led us into a mostly empty storeroom with a ceiling that was at least two stories high. The room backed up to an alley by way of an oversized garage-style rolling metal door. Boxes and crates lined the walls.

In the middle of the room stood a figure. The person turned on kitten heels as we entered, the light from the kitchens behind us falling across the petite woman and the box in her hands.

Sophia.

CHAPTER 25

Monday Evening

What. The. Fuck. I was wholly unprepared for seeing Sophia holding the jewelry box. The box that had caused this whole mess. The box that could turn her into an angel. She clung to it so tightly, her pristine pink nails dug into the distressed wood.

The *tanets angelov* itself was incredibly ordinary, like some scholars believed the Holy Grail would be. All this fuss for some pieces of wood slapped together to hold jewelry. Well, made to look that way, anyway.

"Sophia?" Thane asked, his tone reflecting my incredulous emotions. "How? You never left my side that night."

The corners of her mouth turned up into a devious smile. "No, but you left *my* side. It was easy enough to hide the fae's body and Veronica's hair with a spell until after she showed up and took the fall. You should have listened to me. We could have ascended together."

My nostrils flared out. So that was how my hair showed up at the crime scene. I *knew* I hadn't made such a rookie mistake that night, even if I'd made plenty since.

"Together?" He scoffed. "I had no intention of using the box to cheat my way to the top."

I glanced at him, my anger at being played fading a shade. Maybe I knew people better than I thought. Despite the tension of the situation, a small bit of relief settled over my shoulders. He wasn't a cheater. At this, anyway. I held onto that fact like it was a symbol of hope for our current predicament.

Sophia's eyes narrowed even as she stepped closer to him. "I understand you must feel betrayed and are lashing out."

"I was always going to return the box to Adam." His voice snapped out like a whip. "I just wanted to make sure it didn't fall into the wrong hands."

"And you think mine are the wrong hands?" Sophia laughed as she closed in. "They're better than *hers*."

"Whoa, whoa," I said, holding up my hands in surrender, even though I totally disagreed with her estimation of herself. By illegally obtaining documents for a case she worked on, I had helped the bitch cheat her way up the ladder to earn her wings faster, which turned out to be unnecessary now if she used the box's power. That was way worse than anything I had done. "Don't bring me into this lover's quarrel."

"We are definitely not lovers," Thane said as Sophia placed a hand on his arm. He shook off her touch, his lip curling in revulsion. "I've told you too many times to count, Sophia. You're not my type."

She glared up at him, her green eyes sparkling with anger. "But *she* is?"

He returned her glare with his own fierce gaze. "More so than you."

Good to know I ranked a wee bit higher on the list of acceptable women to date.

"You'd take someone who would murder her own family to your bed?" Sophia took a few steps back, looking aghast. Her world must have been crumbling—a delusional world, but hers nonetheless.

"We aren't sleeping together, and I didn't fucking murder anyone, especially not my brother," I said, wanting to knock her off her feet with a solid sucker punch. I bit the inside of my cheek instead. "Until this week, I thought Maddox committed suicide."

Turning her demented gaze on me, Sophia caressed the box with one hand like a lover would. "You really are stupid, aren't you?"

"I've been making some poor choices lately," I agreed, clenching my fists to keep my fury from escaping.

The whole situation had gotten wildly out of hand and was not going the way I had planned. I never would have imagined Xavier working with a reaper, helping her get her wings, especially when all he got out of the deal was me. I didn't even want to think about what else Sophia might have promised him.

With the situation quickly unraveling, I wasn't sure when to make my attack. It had to be the right moment if I was going to get away with my life and freedom. I should probably make sure Thane escaped, too. Or at least try.

"Wait, why'd you steal the duke's soul?" I asked, my eyebrows pulling together.

"To keep the ignorant fae from talking to another reaper, of course," she said with a dramatic eyeroll, as if souls talking to reapers was common knowledge. For the record, it wasn't. "Anyway, if you'd just looked at your brother's autopsy report a little closer, you'd have seen the taint of magic."

Magic? My mouth parted in shock as I remembered the coroner's call. He had been so apologetic and so sincere for the news he had to give me. He'd had a teenage son of his own to worry about. But he had been a human. He didn't know what he didn't know. I didn't even consider looking at the report myself. Why would I?

The screams of the boys I thought had pushed Mad over the edge echoed through my memories. Each of them had admitted they bullied my brother, confessed that they went too far when they broke his bones. But they had sworn up and down and on all that was holy that he wasn't suicidal. That he had been strong and proud, standing up to them, which only made the bullies angrier. And me, too, when they told me all this, their blood staining the ground beneath them. They described the Mad I knew, not one who would take his own life.

The taint of magic.

Why had someone in the Community wished harm on Maddox of all people? He was proud, sure, but he was also one of the gentlest souls on the planet. And no one in the Community should have known about his existence. They hardly knew of mine back then.

"As charming as this all is," Xavier said, breaking through my trip down memory lane, "I've got dinner plans. Sophia, will you get this show on the road, *por favor*?"

"With pleasure," she said and opened the box. Inside, a tiny winged angel sprang up like a ballerina in a music box.

Thane took a step forward, raising a hand to stop her.

"Ah, ah, ah," Xavier said with a wag of his finger, and a low hissing rose from all the dark parts of the room. Spider-like shapes crawled out of the shadows and climbed down the walls, becoming humanoid figures—vampires.

And if I counted correctly, it was more than one brood this time. I pressed my lips together into a thin line.

Thane obeyed Xavier's command, but I was pretty sure he was calculating the odds like I was. The scales did not tip in our favor.

"While we're at it, let's make sure your little friend stays out of this intimate gathering," the vampire said with a smile. He pulled out a device from his pocket that looked like a TV remote and pushed a button.

A high-pitched squeal resounded in my ear. With a shout, I pulled out the earpiece connecting me to Kit. I glared at him while rubbing my ear. Thane and I were officially on our own.

Sophia chanted in a strange language, reading off something inside the lid. As she uttered the last word, a warm glow grew within the box before spreading down her arms and over her body. The golden light enveloped her entire being in its embrace, and judging by the look on her face, it was an ecstatic feeling. Almost orgasmic.

For the briefest of moments, I was jealous.

Moreso, I was super conflicted about what to do. If I let her become an angel, she'd most likely disappear right after, leaving Thane and me to take the blame, or she would try to ruin my life from her new station in the clouds. Or worse, she would help Xavier even further in some way I hadn't figured out yet.

I'd never watched someone become an angel, and I didn't know what would happen if I interfered. Better to err on the side of caution.

Moving quietly to avoid drawing attention, I drew one of my throwing knives and hurled it at her all in one movement. The blade tumbled through the air with deadly accuracy, aiming for her left eye. I was good.

Unfortunately, she turned out to be better, even during a transformation. Her glowing hand whipped up to catch the knife by the handle, staring at the point of the blade a hair's breadth from touching her eye. The box and the knife dropped to the ground with a clatter as an undulating wave of energy overtook her. She tilted her head back, a scream ripping from her throat as an invisible force pulled her to her tiptoes. Wind swept her hair and clothes upward toward the ceiling.

I raised an arm to protect my face against the dirt and debris that stirred up in the unnatural winds now swirling around her like a vortex. She scrunched over, holding her stomach as if in pain, and that's when I saw them.

Tiny bumps emerged under her shirt on each shoulder blade, pressing against the fabric before ripping through entirely. A pair of wings erupted from her back, growing with each passing breath. The sound was grotesque, both the whimpers and cries coming from Sophia as well as the breaking of bones as her back made room for and formed the imposter limbs. Her body twisted and jerked as she fought to remain on her feet.

When the metamorphosis finished and the glow faded from her skin, Sophia stood straight again. Her face was triumphant as she unfurled new white wings from her back. White wasn't even the right word for them. They were iridescent, with shimmering silver veins trailing down each quill of the feathers. The shimmer spread out into the vanes to reflect the light of the room.

She had become a motherfucking angel.

CHAPTER 26

Monday Evening

Angels were supposed to represent the best of humanity, those who had proven themselves worthy of worship. They were supposed to be divine and allowed to sit at the feet of their god. They were most definitely *not* supposed to be vile cheaters who had zero patience and a delusional vision of how love worked.

So basically, not Sophia.

She turned to Xavier, a triumphant smile on her lips. "Our deal is complete. You've got the Falcon, I've got my wings. Don't bother me again."

Xavier gave her an amused smile and a flourishing bow. "May you enjoy your first flight."

Sophia glanced back at Thane one last time, hope in her eyes. But he didn't budge. Rage simmered beneath his carefully controlled features.

Shaking her head with a look of disgust, Sophia turned toward the door leading out, her wings trailing softly on the ground.

Just as I opened my mouth to yell at her to come back and face me for the blasphemous things she said about me and for blaming this whole mess on me—and maybe call her a few nasty names while I was at it—Xavier lifted a hand and dropped it as if conducting an orchestra. I paused, finding the gesture odd.

Then they moved.

The vampires under his control surged forward at lightning speed to surround the newly made angel, just as another full brood scrambled through the kitchen door. It was hard to describe their movements as anything but that—scrambling. These vampires may have been human once, but now their movements were jerky, sending their limbs flailing. Drool accumulated in their fanged mouths or dripped down their chins as the bloodlust rose to nearly uncontrollable heights.

"What are you doing?" Sophia asked, whipping around to face Xavier. Her face was a mask of fury, but a hint of fear reflected in her green eyes.

"My side of our little bargain included getting you your wings." Xavier sauntered toward her and ran a finger lazily along her feathers. "I never agreed to let you go."

She pulled her wing out of his touch, her upper lip raised in a snarl. "I wasn't yours to begin with. Not like Veronica."

"We'll have to agree to disagree," he said.

Out of the corner of my eye, Thane tensed as I did, both of us ready for a fight.

"Adding an angel to my collection beside a…" Xavier looked at me sideways, a knowing look on his face, "a *shifter* would bring me great pleasure."

My blood ran cold as he locked eyes with me.

He knew what I was. Not just a shifter, he knew I was a phoenix. I had no idea how that was possible considering the Community thought my kind was extinct, but I had no real desire to learn. This show was over.

Faster than it took to shift, which was basically instantaneous, I withdrew two of my throwing knives and launched them in his direction. Both blades were coated with the fast-acting paralyzing poison I loved so much, enough to slow down a bloodsucker, but maybe not a Master—which was why I sent two in his direction.

I hadn't fully expected them to hit their marks, so I wasn't super disappointed when he swatted them from the air without a nick on his skin. But it did provide the *oomph* we needed to get this fight started.

While Thane did his reaper thing with the vamps that closed in on him, his eyes drowning in shadows, I pulled out the derringer strapped to my back beneath my top. With the right aim, the fragmented bullets containing wooden pellets were capable of killing the fools stupid enough to follow their master into this fight.

Good thing I had the right aim.

Shooting at moving targets was much more difficult in real life than movies made it seem. But I'd had years of practice in my bird form catching bugs and fish and whatever else I could find for sustenance, predicting my prey's movements with their telltale signs. I had also spent my entire childhood and teen years training every day to fight in human form.

They say it takes ten thousand hours practicing something to master it, and that was me—with guns, knives, and kicking ass.

Mastering a skill didn't mean I was perfect. Mistakes still happened, but they were fewer and farther between. With that in mind, I chose not to get too upset when the wood-filled bullet I shot at the third vamp didn't kill him. Or her. I didn't really care much right then to stop and ask for gender clarification.

When the vamp was practically in my face and I could smell the rot coming from deep inside its open mouth, I pulled the trigger again, aiming down its throat. Saliva dripped down its fangs. As the bullet exploded and the pellets found its heart, the vampire's body seized. Its face contorted into a death mask, only it wouldn't remain long enough to be preserved. A second later, the undead creature's body crumbled into dust, and its bones fell to the ground.

The derringer wasn't as useful with multiple vamps all trying to get at my neck at once, so I shifted into falcon form. Raking my talons across the closest vampire's face, I swooped up toward the storeroom's high ceiling before turning and diving back at the brood. I slashed at anything I could reach with my razor-like talons, skin and bone shredding beneath my clawed toes. Shrieks of pain motivated me further.

On my next swoop up and out of the way, I saw Sophia was cornered. She was trained to fight as well as any reaper, but she wasn't just a reaper anymore. She had gained new abilities she hadn't been taught to use, not to mention big ass wings that appeared to be more detrimental to her defense moves than helpful.

For now, I would let her fend for herself. She was a good distraction for a group of the bloodsuckers, which would keep them off Thane and me. That reaper appeared to be doing just fine on his own, having whipped out his scythe at some point and wielding it as gracefully as if he were simply dancing.

I dive-bombed again, aiming to maim. If I could injure enough of them before their healing ability kicked in, I might have a chance... But a chance at what? I wasn't sure yet.

As my talons slashed through more flesh, my thoughts distracted, a clawed hand reached up to grab my feet, holding me in place despite my sudden frenzy to escape. I shredded the vamp beneath me with talons and beak. Another vampire skittered close and threw a net over my feathered body. I screeched in defiance. They had teamed up.

I fell to the ground in a feathery heap thanks to all my thrashing. After shifting back to human form, I managed to snatch a knife out of my boot and cut through the netting. I scrambled back to my feet, victorious, only to get knocked something fierce on the back of my head.

I stumbled forward with my hands outstretched, ready to stop my fall if I kept going down. A hard boot connected with my stomach. The breath whooshed out of me, and I collapsed to my knees.

Another attack was imminent, but it was also really hard to breathe. My vision had gone a bit swirly after the blow to the head. Had I been fighting humans, neither hit would have me on the ground, but vamps had inhuman strength like most of the Community species. I was pretty sure that kick broke a rib or two if the level of pain could be trusted.

I put one foot back on the ground to stand and looked up, only to see a frying pan coming straight at my face.

CHAPTER 27

Monday Evening

I threw my arm up to block the blow with a resounding bang and snatched the pan out of the vampire's hands.

"Really? A frying pan of all things?" I was sure there was a sexist joke in there somewhere but fighting made thinking it through to the punchline a tad more difficult.

I used the pan to bash the creature over the head, then spun in a circle, holding the kitchen implement out in front of me. Somehow, the move worked. The vampires surrounding me jumped back to avoid the makeshift weapon. Women really did know how to use frying pans better.

Ah-ha, there was the joke.

If nothing else, at least I could wield it better than the undead.

An idea sprang to mind. I grinned, somewhat maniacally I was sure, and pulled the flames living within me out and into the pan. The bottom ignited with an instant inferno like a grease fire. Bloodsuckers hissed and drew back, but I didn't give them time to think through the new threat. I jabbed at the closest one. A droplet of liquid fire jumped from the pan and onto what was left of the creature's stringy hair.

The flames engulfed the vampire's body within seconds. It screamed and, with arms outstretched, went running for the door. I wasn't really sure where the vamp thought it was going to go, but it clearly never learned to stop, drop, and roll. I wasn't going to complain, though, because that one set two other vampires on fire in its haste. All three became nothing but ash and bones a few moments later.

Through the smoke, I caught sight of Xavier sitting cross-legged on a couple of wooden crates. Not even bothering to get his hands dirty. I would fix that.

Using the flaming pan to keep the other vamps at bay, I strode toward the Master Vampire. He smiled at me as I approached—the nerve.

"You're even more beautiful fighting than I imagined," he said.

"And you're a dead man," I said, holding the pan with two hands like I would a baseball bat, ready to swing. "For real this time."

Xavier threw back his head and laughed.

As expected, one of his minions attacked me from the side. I swung with all the strength I could put behind it—not with the flat cookable side, but with the edge. The heat of the metal and the swing's force meant the pan sliced right through the creature's neck. Its head flopped to the ground, followed by dust as its body disintegrated, leaving nothing but a deteriorating bone pile.

The corner of my lips turned up as Xavier stopped laughing. He slowly lowered his feet to the ground and stood.

Sophia cried out, but I couldn't turn to look just yet. If I did, I might lose my own head. Thane chanted somewhere in the background, but I had to tune it all out to focus on the threat in front of me. I tightened my grip on the pan's handle. A Master Vampire didn't become a Master solely based on age.

Oh no, it was a title earned through blood, sweat, and tears—mainly of their victims. A vampire had to prove himself or herself to the Vampire Kings and Queens by defeating and draining all their opponents in the Blood Trials. Like most of the non-vampire Community, I didn't know much more about the trials except that I most definitely did not want to witness one. Grueling and brutal didn't even begin to cover what they endured.

The ancient man in front of me, the undead creature made of nightmares and unimaginable horrors, had likely killed more people than I could count, and with a savagery I couldn't fathom. While I didn't know much about Xavier Garcia and his past, I did know what I was. And right now, I was fucking *pissed*.

"Are you ready to become mine, little bird?" he asked, his voice quiet but deep with threat.

"If I liked my men dead, then sure." I shrugged, then grinned as my comment sliced through him, the grin making him even angrier. A flush appeared on his cheeks, and his expression darkened.

He might have been a vampire, but he was also a man—a man who had grown up and lived through a world that saw women as weak and inferior for centuries. Just as I predicted, he wasn't ready for women to be his equals or his betters.

And he certainly wasn't ready for *me*.

"Do you always have to get your women through coercion and deception?" I taunted. "Do they beg you for more of their own accord or only because you demand it of them?"

"I look forward to breeding you like the bitch that you are," he growled.

The blood drained from my face, and I nearly lost all my nerve with his words. Breeding me?

I didn't have long to consider his meaning, which was probably a good thing in the grand scheme of things.

He snarled at me and lunged. As soon as his lip had curled, I pulled out my inner fire, engulfing myself in flames. I had trusted my instinct that said he had never dealt with a phoenix face-to-face before, and that trust paid off. The fire wouldn't burn me, only make it incredibly tricky for Xavier to get his claws near me until I used it all up.

I allowed myself to grin again as he backpedaled to keep from colliding with me. Unlike the inferno I created in the DEA's garage, a feat which required one giant burst of power, I only needed a thin, continuous trickle of magic to keep myself aflame this way.

It wouldn't last forever, though.

His elbow caught the outer edge of the fire, and he hissed as he drew back, his shirt smoking. I moved toward him, brandishing the pan in front of me. He stepped to the side, and we circled each other, searching for an opening. I jabbed at him a few times, trying to find his weak spots, but he twisted away or knocked my attempts aside. Steam rose briefly where the fire licked his skin.

A sharp pain pierced through my calf, and I almost lost my grip on my pan from the unexpected attack. I yelled and kicked out, but the vampire attached to my leg held on despite rapidly catching on fire.

I looked back to Xavier, whose pupils and irises bled red as he telepathically called his creations to him. As their maker, he maintained a mental link with each and every one of them. He smiled, a devilish smile that spoke volumes. I had underestimated him as much as he did me.

The vampires not otherwise engaged in a fight attacked me all at once, disregarding the fire as if it didn't exist. Heedless to what the flames did to their bodies, they clung to whatever limb or part of me they could catch in their claws. I collapsed to my knees under their weight, losing the hold on my magic. The flames snuffed out, leaving nothing but smoke and dust behind as the fire took its fatal toll on the vampire brood.

As claws ripped into my stomach, my neck—every inch of me—I screamed and fell to the ground. They were tearing me apart, eating me. The pain seared through me like the burning of ice when it touched bare skin. Slurping and sucking and rending filled my ears, and my vision started to blur. I lost the will to fight back as they drained me of my life force.

I wasn't the praying type, typically reserving my gods' names for emphasizing a colorful frustration. But now, I called out to Rozanica, she who made up the three fates, asking for her mercy. I cried out for Ognebog's flames to quench their thirst upon my enemies. I prayed to Dazhbog, the sun god who eventually called all my kind home, begging that he not let this be my time.

I had more to accomplish, more to uncover about Mad's death. If nothing else, I didn't want to give Xavier the satisfaction of being right about who and what I was, nor let him see the beauty of my rebirth.

Thane loosed a roar. The entire back wall of the storage room cracked and crumbled, then flew outward.

CHAPTER 28

Monday Evening

Thankfully my head was already turned toward the back, which existed only as a demolished pile of rubble, because I was pretty sure I wouldn't be able to look otherwise. The cement floor was cool against my cheek, but everything else hurt and burned, and not in the fun, exciting way Thane made me feel.

Had his roar just blown out the back wall? Or was this a sign of even more reinforcements? If more vampires had shown up—or something worse—I would face a fate worse than death. Xavier would kill me over and over, any way he could imagine, and I would just keep coming back for centuries because that was my nature.

My body shuddered, both from the thought as well as the massive blood loss. At least the vampires had stopped eating me.

Landing barefoot on the stone-riddled ground, a squadron of angels arrived. Reinforcements, just not for the vampires. Feathers whispered as wings settled against the angels' backs. The angels emanated warmth and peace, a glow encompassing their bodies. I squinted from my place on the ground, trying to make out their features through the nearly blinding light.

As they stepped—or maybe glided, I wasn't able to tell if their feet moved—inside the storage room, the glow receded to form a simple halo around each head. The rest of their features remained human, besides the whole wing thing.

How funny. I thought it had been Thane's roar that busted out the wall, but it was just fucking fantastic timing by the angels. Maybe they had been waiting for that moment, just sitting outside playing cards in the air until someone said, "Oh, that would make a great entrance."

I wanted to giggle at the nonsensical thoughts swirling through my mind. Except I was going numb, and my body didn't respond to the humor. A sticky warmth replaced the coolness of the cement beneath my cheek.

Now that the light no longer hindered my view, although a hazy film grew as my body shut down, I counted only eight angels. Less than a full squadron meant the rest were outside, probably watching the restaurant's exits. I laughed at Xavier's stupidity and demise, but only a bubbling cough came out. Blood dribbled down my cheek to join the growing puddle beneath my head.

Even though I hurt—beyond hurt, I yearned for death to ease the mind-shattering pain, wanted to close my eyes and let it all go—I couldn't die just yet. I needed to see Xavier on his knees, begging for mercy when they took his head and blew away his ashes.

And Sophia? I wasn't sure what they would do to a reaper who cheated her way to wings, but I was excited to find out. Excited as I could be while dying anyway.

First things first. Dying could wait.

"Not quite what I expected," one of the angels said as he stepped forward, ahead of the rest. It was the same angel who had chased me through the skies before, the one with the sandy blond hair and who had turned out to be Thane's boss.

Adam. The halo suited him.

His sharp gaze took in Sophia. Thick iron chains wrapped around her and dug into her flesh and wings as she struggled to get back to her feet. No wonder she had cried out. Under Adam's gaze, the vampires holding her let go and stepped back. Glaring at her captors, she shrugged off the chains, which fell to the floor with a loud clanking. She turned back to the other angel.

"Adam, I had to activate the *tanets angelov*," Sophia said, holding her head high. "Ascension was the only way to fight off the Master Vampire and his broods."

Xavier laughed, once again perched on the stack of boxes, but motioned to Adam to speak. As if the vampire had any say in the matter. Centuries might have sharpened his features into a thing of beauty, but ugly narcissism was alive and well in his death.

"Thane?" Adam asked.

"Sophia has been working with Xavier to steal the box," the reaper explained, brushing ashes from his arms and shirt, but otherwise unscathed. "She killed Broderick, stole his soul, and placed the blame on Ms. Neill, then me."

Adam nodded thoughtfully, eyeing me and the pool of blood surrounding me. He wasn't the only one, either—the newer vampires were getting restless with the thick scent of food in the air.

Don't rush on my account. I'm just dying over here.

"He lies," Sophia practically hissed. Scrapes and slashes marred her porcelain skin, and she had lost the little clip she wore to tame the front of her short auburn hair.

"Unfortunately for you," Adam said, refocusing his intense gaze on Sophia, "Thane has been working undercover to reveal the real killer. I had a suspicion it was someone within our ranks once Ms. Neill found herself a target. And now we know that someone was you."

"You don't think *she's* capable of committing such a crime, but you have no issues believing I am?" Sophia spit out.

"That's correct." His gaze fell on the discarded and forgotten jewelry box. "Such a waste."

"I can explain everything," she said, her voice trembling as two angels stepped toward her.

"That won't be necessary." The angel let out a sigh. "Your extracurricular activities of hiring those with skills like Ms. Neill have not gone unnoticed, but I hoped you would have learned a better way after partnering with Thane. Even angels can be proven wrong."

Oh, shit. Little Miss Sophia was a far naughtier girl than I gave her credit for.

Adam didn't move a hair on his holy head, but the other two angels led her by the arms out of the storage room and took to the skies. Her pleading cries echoed into the night. Two more angels spread their wings and joined the flight. I wanted to ask what would happen to her. Nothing like this had occurred in any recent memory.

Adam and Xavier stared at each other, a showdown of wills. I wanted to giggle again at the absurdity of an angel and a vampire facing off, but I also didn't want to hasten my death by offending an angel. I needed everyone to leave first, then I could die in peace.

"Technically," Adam said at last, "according to Community laws, you did nothing wrong."

Xavier smiled, allowing his fangs to show. "I'm glad we can agree on that."

Thane stepped forward, holding up a finger. "If I may?"

The angel nodded.

"He planned to take Sophia with him against her will," the reaper explained. "Adding her to his so-called collection. Along with Ms. Neill."

I wanted to also add that the Master Vampire had intended to use me to create a little phoenix brood of his own. Like all dead creatures, vampires were sterile, so I had no idea with whom or what he had planned to make it happen. My body was already doing enough shuddering all on its own, but I attributed one of them for that last horrific thought.

Thane's gaze moved to me and his eyebrows drew together. He may have been concerned about me, not knowing about my unique ability, but he wouldn't dare speak out of turn in front of his superior. Reapers were far too well-trained for that, especially now that I knew he was working undercover.

What a sneaky little devil. Or wannabe angel was more accurate, I guess.

Adam regarded the Master Vampire, his gaze thoughtful. "Is that so. And how many others do you have in your collection against their wills and against the laws of the Community?"

Wisely, Xavier kept his mouth shut.

I let out a sigh. Actually, it turned out to be my last breath. My heart slowed until it stopped. *Fuck.* I was going to have to reveal myself to everyone in this room. My body would do it even if I commanded it not to.

Adam must have heard my sigh, because he turned to an angel near him and said something under his breath. Or maybe my hearing was failing. My eyesight was making everything dark, too hard to see distinct shapes.

"Veronica!" Thane shouted in the distance.

An angel knelt before me, close enough to see a kind smile on her face through the shadowy haze. She laid her hands on my head and my heart.

I smiled back and died.

CHAPTER 29

Wednesday Morning

Movies and TV shows always showed people waking up after a near-death experience in a hospital bed. They would open their eyes to find the warm rays of the sun falling across their face, mountains of bouquets and cards covering the room, or some other nice shit like that.

Yeah, not so much for me. Instead, I had the pleasant experience of waking up to a flashlight's blinding light as someone lifted my eyelids.

"What the hell?" I asked, scrambling to get away from the glare.

"Oh, sorry," a female voice said. "I thought you were still out. Just checking your vitals."

I sat up and blinked rapidly, trying to clear the white image impressed on my vision. When it finally faded, I discovered I was in my bed at my little apartment near the coffee shop. An angel with opalescent, pinkish-white wings peeking out behind her back and long, curly red hair sat next to me on the bed. She smiled, but all I noticed were her blue lagoon-colored eyes.

"Wow, your eyes are *so* pretty," I said.

She laughed and patted my hand. "I think you're doing just fine. Glad to see you moving around again."

"Again?" I squinted at her, trying to remember if she was at the restaurant. And then I realized I didn't even know what day it was or how I got to my apartment. I hadn't actually died or else I'd still be in the storeroom, reborn from Dazhbog's flames. Naked, too, which would have made for a memorable moment.

The angel squeezed my hand. "I've been assigned to look after you since your brother's passing. The last phoenix is a rare and highly prized jewel that does not deserve a cage."

My heart constricted, and my eyes grew moist with a sudden onslaught of tears. Angels knew of my existence, of course; they knew every Community member's species and abilities. But I hadn't had any clue I was being "looked after." The fact didn't make me scared or angry, it made me feel something close to loved. I had been protected when I thought I was all alone.

"Don't let that frighten you," she said, misunderstanding my expression. "I don't follow you around all day and night, although I probably should with your recent track record. I just do my best to keep an ear out for happenings that may affect you. I'm sorry I failed this time around, but I won't let it happen again."

Even if she did watch me day and night, I knew she wouldn't be able to involve herself in any of my extracurricular activities. Angels weren't law enforcement that way, that's what the reapers were for. Sophia's misbehavior must have warranted a special intervention.

"But don't worry, your secret is still safe," she continued. "I was able to heal you enough before your heart stopped and your nature had a chance to take over. I'm Jessa, by the way."

"Hi. Thane?"

"Oi, vey," she said with a roll of her eyes. "If you two had just come to us before facing Xavier, all of this could have been handled with far less bloodshed."

I stared at her, unable to breathe. Had something happened to him after I blacked out?

Jessa let out an exasperated breath. "He's back at headquarters filling out the never-ending reports as part of his punishment for not following Adam's orders. He was supposed to report to Adam as soon as he learned anything about the *tanets angelov*." She grinned, a tiny gleam appearing in her eyes. "I think he was trying to impress you. He's been asking to see you so much he's starting to annoy Adam."

"How long has it been?"

"Almost two days."

I leaned back against my headboard right as Kit walked in, carrying a steaming mug. The deliciously earthy-yet-alsocitrusy scent of my favorite coffee blend wafted beneath my nose.

"Oh look, you're alive," Kit said with zero humor in her voice. Jessa slid off the bed and gave us some space.

Kit set the mug on the bedside table, proving herself to be the metaphorical angel I knew her to be, and enveloped me in a tight hug. For anyone who knew Kit, that was an unusual move. She was not a touchy-feely kind of girl. But I supposed when her best friend survived near-enslavement by a Master Vampire, she would make an exception.

I returned her hug. "I'm glad you're here. Is Tony alive?"

"He's going to be fine." She pulled back to look me in the face and smiled—another rarity. Guilt clenched at my heart. I must have really scared her.

Along with that piece of awesome news, she and Jessa took turns catching me up on what I missed since my untimely near-death two days ago. Xavier had been taken in for questioning, obviously. The angels then raided his condominium and found his collection of Community members. Some were on the brink of death like me. Some were already in pieces. His trial was set a week from now, and I would for sure be going.

Neither of them would speak of Sophia. Kit because she didn't know anything, and Jessa because she claimed she couldn't. Divine laws and politics and all. At some point during my arguing with the angel as I tried to dig out the details, she gave a brief shudder, her wings partly spreading. She stood and headed for the door.

"Hey Kit, I need your help with something." She didn't wait to see if my friend would listen before she turned and left the room.

Kit and I exchanged a confused glance. I must have really pissed her off pressing for information. Kit followed her out because one does not say no to an angel.

My eyelids grew heavy, so I decided it was time to rest again. I really wished I was in my penthouse, but I assumed me waking up here meant the other location was still a secret. A minor relief as I laid down and closed my eyes.

Something disturbed the air, and I caught the light scent of cardamom. I peeked an eye open. Thanc leaned a shoulder against the doorframe, staring at me.

"Why're you being a creeper?" I rolled over onto my side to face him.

"You need rest." He pushed himself off the door and moving to the seat beside the bed.

Someone had carried the chair in from the kitchen, probably Jessa during her two-day stay. Unless other angels had relieved her at some point. So many people could have been watching me sleep without my knowing. Ugh.

"Apparently I've been sleeping for two days," I said. "I should probably make myself useful."

He smirked, the image sending tickles through my belly. "Nah, take advantage of this downtime. You're going to be weak for a while, anyway."

I wanted to jump right out of that bed and show him how weak I wasn't, except the weariness in my muscles and bones refused to cooperate. Although it might be fun to try. He'd have to catch me in those big, strong arms and...

My gaze drifted up to his face, where he raised a knowing eyebrow in my direction. I was biting my lip as I stared at his body. Damn it.

"What?" Ignorance. Always feign ignorance.

He shook his head and chuckled. "Adam wanted me to tell you that the DEA has officially cleared your reputation, and the Community has been notified."

I sighed in relief, even though it still meant both my real name and my alter ego had been outed through this whole fiasco. I would have to figure out how to keep getting contracts, though I had enough funds to take a few years off. Maybe it was time for a career change again.

At least Isaac hadn't fired me from The Morning Grind yet. Kit's fake doctor's note had me out with the flu for a week. Lucky me, since now I had to recover for real.

"On behalf of all the angels and the agency," he continued, "Adam wanted me to express his gratitude for bringing the real killer to justice and returning the *tanets angelov*." He grinned at me. "He also wanted me to thank you and Kit for exposing the DEA's need for better security at headquarters."

"You can tell him he's very welcome," I said, trying not to sound too smug. "It was the least we could do."

"Lastly, he wanted to make sure I mentioned that none of this would have happened if you hadn't tried to take on more than you could handle."

I sat up at that, blonde waves tumbling around my shoulders. I didn't even care about bedhead right now. The short hairs on the back of my neck practically bristled with my rising temper. "You've got to be kidding me. I was doing just fine until a nefarious, morally corrupt reaper with plans to cheat her way to the top got involved."

"Except you were going to give the box to a Master Vampire," Thane pointed out.

His gaze slipped down from my face to take in my silk pajama top. The tiny bit of material showed off quite a bit of my tanned skin and lack of a bra. I preferred to sleep in fabrics that made me feel sexy, and silk did just that, so it was kind of all I owned. Heat rose in my cheeks, as well as a few other places.

Maybe the silk worked a little too well right about now.

"You know, no one felt the need to tell *me* I was being protected all along," I said, still bristling despite my distracted thoughts. "Besides, the box never would have gotten to Xavier. You people would have intervened. Tell Adam if he were a faster flier, he could have caught me and filled me in."

Thane laughed, the sound sending shivers of desire up my back. "He wasn't chasing you in earnest. He just needed it to look that way to anyone in the agency if his suspicion turned out to be true. Which it did."

I huffed and slid my bare legs off the side of the bed. Now he was going to get the full view of my nightwear, and he would just have to deal with the consequences on his own time.

His eyebrows drew together. "Where are you going?"

"Some of us still have bodily functions to deal with," I grumbled as I heaved myself to my feet. The world spun, and I nearly tipped over until steady hands righted me.

"Angelic healing can come with some unpleasant aftereffects," he said, his warm breath much too close to my cheek.

I turned my head to look at him, our faces mere inches apart. Everything in my body screamed at me to kiss him, strip him, ride him, while my mind yelled at me to stay away from dead guys. This very tempting specimen of a man wanted to become an angel, and therefore not available. As off the market as one could get.

But then, he wasn't an angel *yet*. We could have some fun in the meantime. No one said anything about long term, and he was only, like, kind of dead. Not dead-dead.

At that moment, a new aftereffect of healing by angel made itself known. I turned and threw up on the floor at his feet.

CHAPTER 30

Friday Morning

Another two days later, Jessa finally allowed me out of my apartment. Chances were the angels would be keeping a close eye on me again, but at least I didn't have to deal with anyone hovering at my side. I needed some time to myself, and a walk to *el Mercado Sombra* sounded like the perfect solution.

As usual in Miami, it was sunny, hot, and humid. My kind didn't mind the heat, so I strolled down the sidewalk in flip flops, hands in the pockets of my loose-fitting linen shorts, and enjoyed the sounds and scents of the city. I had faced a Master Vampire and a reaper gone rogue and survived. Sure, it had taken some divine healing, but I wouldn't have died—not the way everyone else did.

Xavier might have known the only way to kill a phoenix, but I'd never know if he did, and what was done was done. I wasn't sure I cared to know, anyway, even if the thought would likely haunt my nightmares for months.

I'd only been reborn once before, but it wasn't exactly a pleasant experience. As part of the ceremony to activate my rebirth ability and allow my parents' return to the sun, their ashes had to merge with mine—except I was the only one to rise again. I knew they had tried to explain the importance behind the ceremony, but I tuned them out in my anger. I had followed their directions one last time, then moved along with my life.

I wasn't as angry at them anymore now that I knew Maddox didn't die by suicide. Instead, I turned that anger on myself and whoever in the Community was responsible for his death. I would spend the rest of my life tracking that person or people down, avenging my brother, and making sure they deeply regretted their decision for years to come. Unless I killed the killer in the process.

Only time would tell.

The taint of magic, Sophia had said. As far as I knew, only the angels were aware of our true nature, and they had that info pretty well-guarded. Xavier had to have been an anomaly. So, if someone killed Mad, it wouldn't have been because he was a phoenix. But why the hell would someone want to murder a sixteen-year-old boy?

I shook my head, sighing as I pushed open the door to the piano shop. The little bell jingled above my head. I needed to get my hands on Mad's file, which meant reaching out to Thane without drawing any unnecessary attention. As I pictured the reaper's face, a tiny shiver of excitement slithered down my spine. He hadn't seemed too grossed out by my vomiting at his feet, but I hadn't seen him since the incident either.

Was he just not that into me? I would have thought a dead guy would be okay with bodily fluids. The heat swarming through my body snuffed out with the apparent snub. His loss.

"Heya, Tony," I called out when I caught a glimpse of the man's bald black head glistening in the light behind the lid of his favorite piano.

The Community healer who had rushed to the hospital did her job well. Tony was back on his feet a day after the attack, before I even came to. Not a sliver of a scar would remain. Magic was some powerful stuff. I was glad to be back in his store without fear of arrest, or worse. I just hoped I would be able to look at him again someday without also seeing the image of his shredded throat.

"Hey there, baby girl. Me, too." His eyes were sad as he winked at me behind his spectacles. A telepathic gift could be both a blessing and a curse.

I wrapped my arms around the back of his shoulders and neck, hugging him tight as he continued to play something jazzy. I didn't know the tune, but it spoke to my spirit and soul, calling me to dance. Tony rested his cheek against my arm, and we swayed together for a few moments while his fingers moved across the keys in their own dance.

After kissing the top of his head, I let go and continued on to the back room. If I stayed any longer, I would start crying with the thought of how close I came to losing him.

I ducked through the curtain, and the magic whispered my name as it accepted my presence into the market.

The winding street was as busy as ever on a Friday. I kept my gaze fixed on the ground to avoid any stares as I headed toward the computer lab. My identity as the Falcon had been outed by the reapers when they tried to track me down. The angels knew I wasn't guilty (of this particular case, at any rate), but they had to play along to keep the real killer—also known as Sophia Clark and one of their own—from figuring out they knew better.

Nothing like being a decoy to catch a rogue reaper.

I clearly didn't need the secrecy the magical firewalls provided anymore, but the lab was the only place I could dig into Mad's death without anyone noticing. That was the goal, anyway. I didn't have any clues pointing to who killed him or why, and I didn't want to take any chances with someone covering anything else up if they caught wind of my snooping.

As soon as I logged into the system, a notification popped up with a new message. Make that a dozen new messages. I opened the first one:

Dear Ms. Neill,

I hope you don't mind me reaching out. I'm sure you're swamped with requests, but I would like to hire you to locate a family heirloom. Please let me know if you're available.

With hope,

Dr. Eduardo Blanco

One by one, I opened the emails, my mouth hanging open in surprise. They were all like that, requests for help. Some for finding items or people, some for more questionable wishes. One even asked me out on a date. I bookmarked that one. Maybe I would have better luck with this whole online dating thing.

A grin pulled at my lips. I leaned back against the chair and placed my hands behind my head, lacing my fingers together.

Being outed as a Master Acquirer had its pros after all.

Thanks for reading!
*Please consider adding a short review on **Amazon** and/or*
***Goodreads** to let other readers know what you thought.*

I love to get to know my readers. You can reach me on Facebook, Instagram, or Twitter **@stephaniemirro**. Sign up for my mailing list to get new release information, special deals, giveaways, become a part of my ARC team, and more. I look forward to hearing from you!

www.stephaniemirro.com

Veronica's story continues in…

WINGS

OF

DEATH

THE LAST PHOENIX: BOOK TWO

GLOSSARY

Adam Larue – Archangel of Miami

Albert Renauldo, Dr. – human plastic surgeon; owns Star Island mansion

Anthony "Tony" – piano shop owner; friend of Veronica

Broderick Ó Faoláin – fae duke; *deceased*

Dazhbog – phoenix sun god and primary deity

Death Enforcement Agency – also known as the DEA; agency of the human world that keeps the Community safe

Drystan Neill – father of Veronica; *deceased*

El Mercado Sombra – also known as the Shadow Market

Enrique Alvarez – human street musician

Giovanni "Joe" Facchini – fae regular of The Morning

Grind; friend of Veronica

Isaac Davidson – manager of The Morning Grind; boss of Veronica

Jessa – healing angel

Katherine "Kit" Parker – natural born witch; best friend of Veronica

Luciana Pérez – natural born witch; owner of The Witch's Brew shop in *el Sombra Mercado*

Maddox "Mad" Neill – brother of Veronica; *deceased*

Manuel – owner of food truck in *el Sombra Mercado*

Mokosh – phoenix earth mother goddess

Ognebog – phoenix god of fire

Rhiannon Neill – mother of Veronica; *deceased*

Rogelio Diaz – natural born warlock; deep in his cup somewhere

Rozanica – three phoenix goddesses of fate

Sophia Clark – grim reaper agent of the DEA

Thane Munro – grim reaper agent of the DEA

The Morning Grind – a DC-based coffee shop in Miami; Veronica's day job

Veronica "V" Neill – the last phoenix

Xavier Garcia – Master Vampire of Miami

ACKNOWLEDGEMENTS

There are so many more people involved in writing a book than I ever would have imagined. This book is all the better because of each and every one of these people. Anything you dislike or find wrong with the book, it's probably because I made some sort of "executive decision" as "The Author" (aka, I didn't listen).

To my parents, who always pushed me to follow my dreams no matter how difficult, *thank you*. To my husband, who did more than his fair share of chores and parenting while I wrote, edited, and marketed, *thank you*. To my kids, who tried their hardest to let me work even though work is a foreign concept to them still, *thank you*.

To my editors, Renee Dugan, D.F. Jones, and Ana Morgan; my critique partners, author Martin Wilsey and Tom Mirro; and my beta readers, Leilani, Kimmie, Jessica, Shelley, Michelle, Alisha, Rachel, Devon, Lauren, Erica, Vicki, and Erin, *thank you*.

To my mentor, author Rebecca Hamilton, who

provided invaluable advice developing this series, *thank you*.

To Claire Holt of Luminescence Covers, who brought Veronica to life with this stunning cover, *thank you*.

To all my family and friends, who showed their support in so many ways—asking how writing was going, becoming Patrons on Patreon, and following me on all things social media—*thank you*.

To you, my dear reader, for picking up this book and making it through to the end, *thank you*.

My life is forever changed because of each and every one of you.

ABOUT THE AUTHOR

Stephanie Mirro's lifetime love of ancient mythology led to her majoring in the Classics in college, which wasn't quite as much fun as writing her own mythology stories as she did growing up. But that education, combined with an overactive imagination, being an active fantasy reader, and having a vampire obsession, resulted in the *Immortal Relics* series.

Born and raised in Southern Arizona, Stephanie now resides in Northern Virginia with her husband, two kids, and two furbabies. This thing called "seasons" is still magical.

Made in the USA
Monee, IL
29 March 2021

64167569R00146